ELIOT GRAYSON

THE ALPHA CONTRACT

MISMATCHED MATES SERIES

Cover by Fiona Jayde

Published by Smoking Teacup Books
Los Angeles, California
ISBN: 9798848216684

Author's Note

Brook's genetic condition involves seizures as one of the symptoms, but Hensley's Syndrome is entirely imaginary and affects only were-wolves. It is not meant to reflect the symptoms, diagnoses, or experiences, in general, of real humans with epilepsy or seizures with other causes. Anything that seems unlikely can be ascribed to artistic license (he's a werewolf, so he has a very different physiology). That said, I have several people close to me who have been diagnosed with various forms of epilepsy, and I did consult them to make sure my descriptions of Brook's experiences were somewhat grounded in what a real person might subjectively (key word being might!) feel under similar circumstances.

That said yet again…since I have a soapbox and I might as well use it, there are a variety of organizations that help families with children who have epilepsy or other seizure-causing illnesses, and I've listed two below that I know (from talking to some friends whose kids have gotten help from them) are legit and do really good, worthwhile things in the world, in case any of my lovely readers would like to learn more about how to help.

Epilepsy Foundation: epilepsy.com
Mowat-Wilson Syndrome Foundation: mowat-wilson.org

Chapter 1

Nothing Wrong with a Few Standards

Three men sat at the bar, none of them the one I'd come to meet—or at least I sincerely hoped so. Two had to be my father's age or older, while the third sported some unholy fusion of a mullet and a man-bun.

No position as a CEO would be worth having to look at that every day.

Let alone worth fucking the individual who'd thought that was a good idea, even the once that forming a mating bond would require. Desperation had its limits.

I shuddered and scanned the rest of the dimly-lit space, poking my glasses farther up my nose. A few men had grouped around the pool table in the back past the bar, but they appeared to be there together, and not waiting for anyone.

Several booths, one occupied by a pair of middle-aged women, the next empty, and—there. A lone man with a pint of beer in front of him, slouched back too far into the seat to put his face in the dim glow of the shaded lamp dangling over the table.

Unless I'd been stood up, and I certainly wouldn't discount the possibility, that had to be him.

And anyway, I'd rather be stood up than have to wait on the guy. Punctuality showed character. I didn't expect much from some seedy alpha douchebag with more cockiness than common sense, someone who'd managed to end up on the run from not one, not two, but *three* packs holding grudges, not to mention a variety of loan sharks, but lateness I simply could not abide.

Again, nothing wrong with a few standards. No man-buns, no mullets, no lack of basic time management skills.

And if it kind of sounded, even to me, as if I were trying to think of reasons to call this whole miserable plan off, well…that wasn't entirely wrong.

The bartender glanced up as I moved away from the door, raising her eyebrows at me in a way that suggested she wondered if I'd come to the wrong place. I'd ditched the tie in the car, but my tailored Italian suit probably cost more than six months' rent on this dingy, smoky hole. She knew I didn't belong here.

That made two of us.

I nodded at her and gestured vaguely toward the guy in the booth, and she shrugged and went back to reorganizing the glassware.

He didn't move as I approached, not even leaning forward to get a better look at me—not that he'd need to, what with the perfect vision all shifters had.

All of them besides me, at least.

Yet another way in which I'd been born shockingly imperfect, along with my barely above-average height and my lack of the stronger werewolf magic that would've made me an alpha. Not that my father had known about all of these faults on the day of my birth, of course. He'd still had hopes, at that point, that I'd become something worthwhile—hopes I'd slowly dashed in the intervening twenty-eight years. He never ceased reminding me of it, particularly on days when I'd accomplished more for the family business interests and the pack than my older alpha brother ever would, even in his arrogant, delusional dreams.

Whatever.

Fuck my father, and fuck Blake, and fuck anyone who thought I couldn't conduct business in a seedy dive as well as in the shiniest board room in downtown Boise.

I lifted my chin and strode the rest of the way to the booth with the same confidence I displayed when doing my job.

Hopefully it'd fool enhanced alpha senses.

"Dimitri?" I said as I stopped at the end of the table.

"Who's asking?" The slight Russian accent suggested I'd found the right man. But his low, raspy tone didn't sound all that welcoming.

Jesus, fuck him too. I hadn't forced him to meet me. Our mutual acquaintance, a seedy fixer I sometimes employed as an investigator, had told me Dimitri Pechorin would be just as pathetically eager to find a way out of his difficulties—well, as I was.

"Brook," I said. Johnny had probably shared my last name too, but damned if I'd announce it in a place like this for anyone to hear. Showing my face was bad enough. "And if you're not here to meet me, then say so and stop wasting my time."

"Wasting *your* time?" He shifted his weight, the booth creaking. I had the impression of someone a whole hell of a lot bigger than me, but my weak eyes wouldn't allow me to focus past the pool of light on the table. "You're the one who set this meeting, Castelli." I flinched, glancing around guiltily before I could catch myself. "So sit down and tell me what the fuck you want."

His voice held a hint of an alpha's command. I gritted my teeth, stiffening my knees as they tried to obey his order, and wished I could tell him to go to hell. The last thing I wanted to do was sit down, now that he'd told me to. But I'd probably attract even more attention standing in front of the table like an idiot.

And I'd spent years obsessing over my situation, and now months stressing over my father's new plans for me, without ever coming up with a better plan than this.

Maybe my father was right, and I didn't have what it took to run our companies, the pack, or so much as a lemonade stand.

I sat down with poor grace, sliding a little ways into the booth but making sure to keep a respectable distance from Pechorin.

Once I'd blinked a couple of times, he came into focus at last.

I blinked again, because I couldn't help it.

Okay, no. He might not have a mullet or a man-bun, and he'd been early for our meeting—and he was obviously an alpha—but there the list of qualifications as a mate ended as suddenly as if it'd run into a brick wall.

Which he kind of resembled himself, actually. His shoulders, anyway.

Rumpled, overly long black hair, the harsh-featured face of a hard man who'd lived a hard life, at least a few days' worth of unshaven beard, piercing gray eyes, and those absurd shoulders straining the threadbare seams of an olive-green Henley with a hole in one sleeve.

He had all the polish of a battered piece of scrap metal I might find in a junk yard—at least, if I'd ever set foot in a junk yard.

And he looked to be well over six feet, probably a good half-foot taller than me, though I'd only know for sure once he stood up.

Alphas did tend to the large, and I needed an alpha for my plan to work, but...no. He'd dwarf me if we stood next to each other, which we'd need to do all the time: at the formal mating reception, in photos, at our public appearances...and any authority I had would be eroded by the comparison between his overt alpha-ness and my lack of it.

Of course, any authority I had with members of my family or with the pack would derive from having an alpha mate in the first place. The less traditional werewolf and human employees of Castelli Industries might view me with respect—because I'd earned it. But their opinions wouldn't matter a damn without my father's willingness to hand over the reins.

A cold, heavy clench caught at my chest. Yeah. And if I showed up with *this* alpha as a mate, my father would laugh in my face.

On the other hand, Pechorin did fulfill the nominal requirement my father had laid down. And he'd be *my* choice, not my father's. If I went along with him and let him choose an alpha from our milieu, someone sophisticated and educated and acceptable, he'd step in and take credit for everything I'd worked for. My father would put him in charge. Between the two of them, my father and his hand-picked alpha, they'd decide I'd be much better off spending my time suitably for an influential alpha's mate: making myself as pretty as possible—not very, in other words—and standing behind him, smiling and keeping my fucking mouth shut.

He'd already strongly suggested a couple of men who'd fit that bill, and I'd started running out of time to put him off. I had to find my own mate if I didn't want one forced on me.

No way to win, except to change the rules of the game.

When Pechorin spoke again, it startled the hell out of me. "You going to keep staring at me, or what?" he demanded.

I swallowed hard. "Excuse me," I managed. "My eyesight's not the best."

"The glasses clued me in," he said, with a hint of sarcasm that made me flush and fidget. He picked up his beer and took a swig, his own sharp eyes, that probably hadn't missed a thing, never leaving my face.

Oh, hell. What did I have to lose, anyway? My father would never put Blake in charge; he cared about appearances, but he cared more about his shareholders' profits. And Drew, my alpha cousin, whom my father had tried to groom for the job and marry to a female alpha with a distinguished pedigree—well, he'd vanished for months, come back mated to a human, and then taken off for California. Even if my father had been willing to overlook all that, Drew had made it more than clear my father could stuff it. Blake would've drawn a hefty salary and fucked off to Hawaii or something, leaving me the de facto boss. And Drew—well, he wasn't an asshole, and he'd have shared the job with me, at least, and listened to me. I could've lived with either of those two options, as much as it would've chafed me to do all the work and never get any of the credit for it.

Now it was either get mated off to someone who'd be in control of me for the rest of my life, leave the family completely…or find my own alpha.

I couldn't go off on my own. Much as my overbearing, unloving family made my life hell, the prospect of being completely alone in the world, cut off and without a pack, chilled me to the bone. I simply couldn't do it. Maybe that made me a coward.

But I couldn't do it. And even if I did bring myself to, it'd mean giving up everything I'd worked for.

I cleared my throat and leaned forward, putting my forearms on the table in a pose that I'd learned, from a lot of tense meetings, looked focused and serious.

"Johnny told me you have unmet financial obligations and some other individuals you'd like to avoid," I said. I'd meant to work up to the point a little more gradually, but the impatience on Pechorin's face and the blunt way he'd spoken to me so far suggested he wouldn't appreciate it. "I have the resources to bail you out of what-ever trouble you're trying to outrun. And I have a personal issue I think you could help me with. I think we could help each other."

Pechorin raised a skeptical eyebrow, and the corner of his mouth twitched up. "I believe you about your resources, but if you really want someone to off your brother, arranging it in person, in a bar, under your real name, is about as stupid as it gets. And I don't think I want to work for someone that fucking reckless."

At *off your brother* I started to choke, and by the time he finished I could hardly hear him over my own wheezing. Kill Blake? Okay, yes, I could see the appeal in the abstract, but...*kill Blake*? He thought I'd had him meet me here to pay him to murder my brother? What the hell had Johnny said to him?

My eyes watered, and I waved Pechorin off as he frowned at me, even though he hadn't made the slightest move to slap me on the back or anything. "I'm fine," I gasped. "Jesus. I'm fine."

Not that he'd bothered to ask. Asshole.

"So that's a no on killing your brother?" Pechorin said nonchalantly. Too nonchalantly? Had that been his terrible version of a joke? Was he fucking with me? Christ, either way I might be out of my depth. "Okay," he went on. "What's your problem, then?"

I stuck a finger under my glasses to dry off my eyelids, not a very dignified maneuver, and blinked him into focus again.

Fuck. This. I'd shoot my shot, and then he could finish his beer while I took off to find a bar with acceptable liquor to drown my sorrows.

"I want to take over Castelli Industries when my father retires," I said baldly—albeit quietly, because I really didn't want to be over-heard. Especially not after Pechorin's voicing of his assumptions. "I've been working my whole life for it. I'm competent. The board respects me—to a point. But I'm not an alpha, and in my family, being an alpha's everything. So I want an alpha mate, someone my father would see as being the real man in charge. In return for financial security, that alpha would stay out of my way and have nothing to do with the actual running of the company."

Pechorin's mouth dropped open, and he froze with his beer halfway to it.

Well, at least I'd managed to make him as speechless as he'd made me. The fact that he could talk about "offing" my brother so casually while the idea of a fake mating shocked him this much struck me as horribly funny, and I had to cough to cover a laugh.

"An alpha mate," he repeated after a second. "Me?" He didn't bother coughing; he started laughing openly, his eyes bright with it. He almost looked handsome for a second. "You want *me* to mate with you? Are you out of your fucking mind, Castelli?"

That hurt a lot more than I'd have thought possible. I didn't know this guy. Didn't care what he thought of me. But I'd already had more doubts than otherwise about this plan—and his mockery cut deep, underscoring how fucking pathetic it was to be here, in this shitty bar on the edge of town, trolling for a random criminal to mate with me for money.

Because no one wanted to do it for free. Anyone who wanted me only cared about my last name and my father's bank account. I'd be paying for a mate one way or the other, and I preferred honesty.

"Yeah, I guess I am," I snapped, and lurched up out of my seat. "Sorry to have wasted your time after all."

Standing up took me out of the circle of light above the table and into the dimness again, and I stumbled over my own feet, not seeing a projecting corner of the booth and knocking my elbow into it painfully.

Cursing under my breath, cheeks burning, I booked it out of the bar as fast as I could, letting the door slam shut behind me.

My face tingled as hot skin met a chill wind, and the barest purplish remains of daylight along with the overcast sky left the parking lot even gloomier than the cigarette butts and blowing trash and dirty gravel would've accomplished on their own.

Fuck this all over again. I needed a drink, and to hide out and lick my wounds for a while.

Maybe I should quit after all. My family couldn't actually force a mate on me, could they? My trust fund from my grandfather meant I'd be able to survive, even if they cut me off financially.

But no. I loved my work. In fact, I didn't do much else. Completely aside from the fact that I burned, with a fire I could hardly contain some days, for the credit I'd earned for all my efforts and disregarded successes.

Shit, shit, shit. No good choices. And this had been my only chance to make a real decision for myself, take some control of the situation. I wouldn't have the courage to try again.

The bar door slammed again behind me as I beeped my car

unlocked and reached for the handle. Pechorin following me? I closed my eyes and took a deep breath, begging any deities listening to grant me enough patience to get away without antagonizing this asshole too much. He could turn me into a smear on the gravel if he wanted to, and since he didn't seem to have any moral issue with murdering my brother, no doubt he'd extend the same level of concern to me.

"Wait up," he said, and I turned around, knowing I'd never make it into the car before he caught me.

Pechorin stopped a couple of feet away, just outside of arm's reach. Tactfully? It seemed hard to believe.

Either way, he didn't present less of a threat because he'd kept some distance. Standing, he towered over me as much as I'd expected, and those shoulders blotted out what was left of the setting sun.

He frowned down at me, face even more harsh and angular in the muted violet glow of twilight, eyes lit silvery opaque.

"You're definitely nuts," he said abruptly. "But that doesn't mean I'm not interested." He swallowed, Adam's apple bobbing, and for a second, something passed across his face that could've been vulnerability. It was gone before I could blink. Surely I'd imagined it. "I need money. Badly. And I can handle the packs that're after me, probably, but I'll run out of luck eventually. The thing is...okay, are you talking about actually mating? Or just pretending to be?"

I only wished it could be pretend. And aside from that, half of me longed to tell him to go fuck himself.

But he didn't sound aggressive or hostile. Maybe I hadn't imagined that flash of something more, or possibly less, than the abrasive arrogance he'd displayed in the bar...

"It'd have to be real," I said, forcing myself to put my feelings aside. This was a business negotiation like any other, dammit. "We'd have to pass muster with a shaman during the ritual at the formal mating reception, if nothing else."

Pechorin mulled that over for a beat. "I don't know about you, but I'm straight," he said at last. "But one fuck with a guy can't be that bad. Lie back and think of England, I guess? At least you can."

A twinge of irritation pinged through me. *I* could? "You could always be the one getting fucked."

Pechorin burst out laughing.

My cheeks flamed. "I may not be a hulking alpha criminal, but that doesn't mean I don't top!"

"Sorry," he said, sounding not even slightly sorry. And that shit-eating grin made me want to punch it off his face. I'd break my hand, but…worth it. Couldn't he have at least reacted to the insult? "You know how bonds work, Castelli. You could bite me, but it might not even take. Also, I'm not doing it, no matter how much you pay me."

"I can't believe you'd casually offer to kill someone and then flat-out refuse to take it up the ass. Your moral compass points in some direction I didn't know existed. And I'd be paying you a lot."

Pechorin shrugged and laughed again. "You'd better be paying me a lot. Doesn't matter. It's off the table."

That didn't surprise me in the slightest, because I knew alphas. He'd rather die fighting off three hostile packs than bend over, no matter how impractical and foolhardy that attitude might be. But still—dammit. I'd had this fantasy of walking into the corporate offices of Castelli Industries with my alpha mate, my bite on his neck, and everyone goggling at how badass I had to be to get this big, tough alpha to submit.

Well, that had always been a long shot.

"Fine," I gritted out. "But we're going to have to have a long talk about the terms and conditions. On both sides. Because maybe I'm going to be the one taking your knot and your bite, but that wouldn't extend to any other aspect of our relationship. I'm in charge. We do things my way. And if you don't agree to that, then there's no point to this."

Pechorin took a step forward, and my bravado drained away like he'd pulled the plug. But shaking knees or not—because fuck, that threatening frown on his already imposing face, and the rest of him looming over me—I stood my ground, lifted my chin, and stared him down.

"Why me?" he asked abruptly, tilting his head and examining me like I was a puzzle he couldn't figure out. A futile effort given his probable intellect. Okay, I was kind of a bitch inside my own head, and I wouldn't have said that out loud even if my father retired on the spot. I wanted to live. "Johnny's not a total scumbag, but he's not who I'd think someone like you would go to if you were looking for a matchmaker. And I'm sure you ran a background check on me. Not to mention what Johnny already knew. So why me? Because I'm disposable? You get what you need, and then I disappear?"

"You…" I choked, my eyes widening. Disappear? First he thought I wanted to dispose of my brother, and now he assumed I'd want to have him killed too? "How fucking cynical *are* you? No! No, I'm not planning on making you disappear! Is that how you operate?"

Okay, stupid question, because his objection to killing Blake hadn't been the act itself but rather my lack of caution in trying to set it up.

I had to cling to the idea that he'd been joking. Otherwise, I might simply run away screaming right now.

"If I need to," he said after a moment. "It's not my first choice." He looked me up and down, slowly and thoroughly. I'd have taken it for a come-on if he hadn't already been so clear that I didn't trip his trigger in the slightest. "Hmm. Yeah, you're more the hostile take-over kind of guy, right? Stab them in the back, or the wallet. Not an honest claw to the jugular."

I flinched, stung and insulted and all kinds of fucking furious. "Fuck you," I snarled. "You don't know me. And mating you and then having you killed? That doesn't sound all that honest to me. Make up your fucking mind, Pechorin."

"You're either really stupid or really brave." A funny little half-smile quirked the corner of his mouth. A real smile this time, though, one that lit up his eyes. "I'm going to guess not stupid, given that you're really good at what you do. I checked you out too before I agreed to this meet," he went on as I opened my mouth. "I may not have gone to an Ivy League, but I'm not a total fucking idiot. So I know you're not dumb. But facing me down like this, when I could rip you to pieces and be gone before anyone could even call the cops? That looks dumb on the face of it, yeah?"

It really, really did. I swallowed hard and tried to sound confident and in control. "But you're not going to." I had to swallow again as he stared at me, gray eyes so hard and unblinking. "Right?" And that came out in a weak quaver. Well, fuck me sideways.

"Right," Pechorin said softly. More softly than I'd thought he could speak. "I'm not. And I'm gonna go with brave. That's not always a good thing." He shrugged. "But fuck it, maybe I'm the dumb one. I'll negotiate. Tell me when and where."

Feeling like I'd lost control of my own actions, like in a dream or a hallucination, I pulled a pen and a business card out of my inner jacket pocket and scrawled the name of a downtown hotel on it, along with my cell number.

"Tomorrow evening, eight o'clock. Send me your number so I can text you the room number tomorrow," I said, and handed him the card. Did I even want to go through with this? I couldn't decide, and it was probably a terrible idea, but I seemed to have built up too much momentum to stop now. Like I'd already jumped off the cliff, and it was too late to do anything but flail my limbs all the way to the bottom. "Don't be late."

Pechorin bared his teeth at me in something like his previous grin, only terrifying. "Hotel room, huh?" He waggled his eyebrows. "Classy. And I can tell you're going to be a barrel of laughs," he said, and turned and walked away.

Just like that. I blinked at his retreating back.

Christ. What the hell had I been thinking?

Chapter 2

Malicious Compliance

"I'm going to need another few grand this month," said one of my least favorite voices in the world.

The spreadsheet in front of me blurred into a meaningless grid, and my hand tightened around the mouse, plastic creaking in my grip as I fought the urge to use that hand to push my glasses up my nose. That move would be guaranteed to bring on a flurry of mockery from my asshole brother. I forced my fingers to loosen. Even a werewolf without alpha strength could wreak havoc on computer components.

"Blake," I gritted out, glancing up and blinking at him. He came into focus, leaning casually against the frame of my office's door, hands stuffed in the pockets of his stupid designer jeans—if you were going to spend that much money that wasn't even yours, wear a suit, dammit, and look like an adult—and with a twisted smirk making his handsome face ugly. At least to me. Plenty of other people seemed to find Blake charming.

Well, they found his bank account and his knot charming.

His knot, and our company's bank account, to which he considered himself entitled.

Asshole.

"So?" he said. "Maybe ten, actually. I thought I'd head to Palm Beach for a few—"

"I could not give less of a fuck about your vacation plans." My teeth had clenched together hard enough to give me an instant headache. "Not that you need a vacation, since you've never worked a day in your life. Also, you have multiple credit cards that get paid off at the end of the month. Use them."

"Dad canceled the black Amex," Blake whined. "The others are maxed out. Ten grand, Creek. Come on. Don't be a dick."

Blood pounded in my temples. The discreet testing I'd had done confirmed that the genetic flaw that had given me my terrible eye-sight and the occasional tonic-clonic seizure wouldn't lead to further issues, like strokes. Especially since I hadn't even hit thirty yet. But it sure felt like one.

Creek wasn't quite as bad as Canal as a replacement for Brook; it didn't near-rhyme with "anal."

Still. My fist itched to connect with Blake's nose. It'd heal within five minutes, faster than my hand would.

That was pretty much all that was stopping me at this point.

Two urges to flatten someone's face in as many days. I was on a roll.

"You already asked our parents, right?" The sheepish horror on Blake's face made me cackle aloud, an unprofessional noise that I choked down almost instantly, afraid it'd carry out of my office. "Oh, too scared to ask? Well, I'm saying no. Ask them. Or fuck off."

Blake's low growl didn't scare me. Even though the spread-sheets still hadn't come into perfect focus, I stared back at them, ignoring the way my brother had completely failed to fuck off.

"Dad'll give me the money," Blake said, low and ugly. "I just didn't want to bother him. Not like you have anything important to do. You'll never have anything important to do around here, because you'll never be able to handle it. You'll never be an alpha."

Now the spreadsheets were nothing more than a haze of red, but I didn't dare look up. I'd lose my cool.

What I had left of it.

"You are an alpha," I managed to choke out. "And you're still useless."

Blake let out something between a huff and a growl, but he finally shoved himself off the door frame and stomped away, letting me get the last word. That actually pissed me off more than a lame retort would have. Like my opinion of him didn't even matter enough to rebut.

Our father probably would give him the money; he'd only canceled the Amex so that Blake would be forced to ask, giving him the opportunity to deliver a lecture. And then once he'd given Blake what he wanted, he'd take me to task for sending my brother to waste his valuable time rather than simply dealing with it on my own—even though he'd planned on seeing Blake about it in the first place.

My headache intensified.

If you can't even handle a simple issue like your brother's finances, Brook, I don't understand why you'd expect more responsibilities.

Or something along those lines. I had a thousand quotes like that embedded in my brain after years of the same old, same old.

That morning I'd been wavering on whether I ought to cancel my meeting with Pechorin. Call it all off. Trying to mold that rough-hewn criminal into an alpha my father would respect enough, while still keeping him from taking charge and fucking me over, felt like such a Hail Mary pass.

And I'd be taking his knot, along with his uninterested contempt, in order to mate with him in the first place.

Bottoming didn't appeal to me, in any sense: in bed, in life, in my personal relationships.

Still better than dealing with Blake on these terms for one more fucking day. Or with my father's dismissive attitude and pressure to mate an alpha of his choosing. Or the board, who listened to my ideas, hemmed and hawed, put off implementing them until the ideal time to do so had passed, and then assigned some other junior executive to put them into practice and take credit for any resulting success.

They kept hoping Blake would suddenly manifest some hitherto unknown talent or aptitude for business, and in the meantime…well, they had complete confidence in my father's ability to run our several companies for decades to come.

My fucking father.

Who'd gone to great lengths to keep the results of his own even more discreet genetic testing secret, knowing perfectly well that the packs we socialized and did business with would see any imperfection, any crack in his perfect alpha façade, as an unforgiveable flaw worthy of shunning. Who might only have another five years, max, before his declining health forced him into retirement, even though he kept up a front of the perfect vigorous alpha, and meanwhile treated me like shit for having the same genetic abnormality he'd passed down to me.

Fucking hypocrite. I had to loosen my grip on the mouse again or risk disintegrating it.

I could take Pechorin's knot. *And* I could keep him in line, damn it all.

With Drew and Blake unavailable and unsuitable respectively, and me mated to an alpha and thus satisfying the traditionalists on the board, my father would be left with no choice but to promote me into his position before his secret came out and our stock prices plummeted into the sub-basement. An alpha and a Castelli would make everyone happy. They didn't have to be the same person to keep up appearances, as my father's mating plans for me proved.

It took half an hour before I could focus again, but I forced myself to keep at it, keep working on this fucking proposal that the board wouldn't even consider if it came from me without an alpha endorsement, until six o'clock on the dot.

The drive home only took fifteen minutes despite rush-hour traffic. My grandparents had established their own upscale version of a pack compound: a gated community with all the bells and whistles. My parents lived in the massive mansion my paternal grandparents had built to dominate the center of it. After coming back from college, I'd tried to argue for living somewhere else, but they'd already had a house set aside and furnished for me.

And like a spineless coward, I'd moved in and had been there ever since.

The hotel room had been a precaution, even though I'd have preferred to meet in my own space: werewolf instinct, to have the home-turf advantage. The gate guard on duty would almost certainly report Pechorin's visit to my mother if he came here, and we needed to be mated or very close to it before my family got a whiff of his existence and the opportunity to throw a spanner in the works.

But I had to get home first: I needed to shower to wash off the stink of anxiety and to dress in something a little more casual, something that'd blend in with the guests of the mid-range chain hotel I'd chosen.

Dark jeans and a sports jacket over a white button-down, I eventually decided, and took a quick survey in the hall mirror on my way back out the door again. The shower had left my short blond hair a little darker, but it looked okay damp, only slightly rumpled.

The navy jacket brought out the blue of my eyes—what you could see of them behind the wire-frame glasses that would've done any accountant proud. Not like stylish ones would've helped make me less of a shocking anomaly. Werewolves who needed vision correction were rare enough that I might well have been the only one west of the Mississippi.

Dressed down by my standards or not, I'd still be in a different zip code from the man I was going to meet.

And I needed whatever edge I could get. Maybe the clothes didn't make the man, but I looked a hell of a lot more imposing sharply dressed. It compensated a little for my not quite six feet of height.

Well, okay. Five foot ten. But close.

Pechorin probably could've intimidated nearly anyone stark naked, I thought with a surge of bitterness.

Of course, that was why I needed him.

I spun away from the mirror and headed for the car before I could talk myself out of it all over again.

By the time I'd checked in and texted Pechorin the room number, I only had half an hour to make sure I had all my ducks in a row. It didn't feel like enough, but within ten minutes my notes on my requirements were all laid out on the table—not in any legally binding format, since I could hardly enforce a contract I didn't want anyone besides the principals to know existed—and I'd put on the provided pot of undoubtedly vile coffee and rehearsed what I needed to say.

The room didn't offer much by way of distraction. I wrinkled my nose at the ugly bedspread and the prints of scenic Idaho mountains on the walls, none of which had more aesthetic appeal in the sunshine pouring through the room's one large window. Since the sun wouldn't set for another hour and a half, at least we'd have natural lighting for this. Somehow, agreeing to a sordid mating-for-money under the dim, pinkish glow of the room's cheap compact fluorescent lightbulbs would've seemed so much sleazier.

At 7:56, the elevator around the corner dinged. I wiped my sweaty palms on the seams of my pants. Showtime.

But then nothing happened. It must have been someone going to another room.

Would he stand me up? He'd shown up yesterday; he'd even been early, although that had to have been more about scoping out the bar and having an edge than about courtesy. And he'd all but agreed to do this. Would he be late on purpose, just to make the point that he wouldn't do what I told him to? To demonstrate his dominance? I grimaced. That kind of petty mind game didn't show dominance; it showed immaturity, but plenty of alphas didn't know the difference.

A sharp rap on the door made me jump. There hadn't been any other sounds from the hallway. I glanced down at my phone.

Eight o'clock on the dot.

That had to have been him in the elevator.

Now I had to wonder: Did malicious compliance show dominance or not?

My mouth quirked in something not quite a smile. It definitely showed a sense of humor, although it came at my expense.

Two could play at that game.

I stood there and watched my phone until it changed to 8:01, and then opened the door. Pechorin raised one eyebrow and stared me down. To my shock, he'd dressed up—by what appeared to be his standards, at least—for the occasion, wearing decent jeans, a black button-down, and a leather jacket. He wouldn't have stood out at all crossing the hotel lobby.

"You're late," I said.

"You looked at the time and waited to open the door," he replied, and sauntered in, forcing me to step too quickly out of the way or get run over. It knocked me off-balance both literally and figuratively, and I stumbled as I shut the door behind him.

A warm, firm hand wrapped around my elbow, a match to the warm, looming presence of him, making me feel hemmed-in and off my game. We hadn't touched before.

We'd be touching a lot if we went through with this. I shivered.

"Careful," he rumbled. "Your depth perception isn't the best, right?"

I jerked my arm away, stumbling again and knocking my shoulder into the wall. "My depth perception is fine," I snapped, lying through my clenched teeth.

"Uh-huh." His skepticism rasped on my already stretched nerves. "I did a little reading last night. You have Hensley's Syndrome. Nearsightedness, poor night vision, bad depth perception, and that's just the eye symptoms. I noticed all of those last night, by the way."

I fell back against the wall like he'd cut my strings, gaping up at him open-mouthed with shock and horror. His raised dark brows and frowning mouth blurred in front of me, and not because of my eyesight. If my heart beat any faster, I'd go into cardiac arrest.

Pechorin stepped toward me, broad shoulders blotting out the light from the window, his heat and alpha pheromones and hard gray eyes filling all my senses.

"Seizures, strokes, spinal deformation—you obviously don't have that last one. Tremors. Your hands were shaking yesterday. Hearing loss, although that doesn't seem to be an issue for you. Seems like the kind of thing you might want to disclose to a potential mate, doesn't it?"

The hypothetical stroke might happen right now, actually. Terror held me rigid against the wall. He was trying to blackmail me. Extort the money I'd have paid him to mate with me without doing anything but threaten to expose me, and by extension, my family.

My fingers went numb and tingly. I could feel the blood draining out of my face, my skin cold and clammy.

"You're out of your mind." My lips barely moved, and the words came out a hoarse whisper. Not very convincing. "I had—an injury. To my eyes. When I was a teena—"

"Bullshit," Pechorin cut in. "Total fucking bullshit. Any injury that left you with intact eyes at all would've healed. Is that the story you tell publicly when people ask about your glasses?"

It was, actually. My parents had come up with the lie and drummed it into me: an accident while using cleaning chemicals during the summer while I'd been at camp and helping clean the swimming pool, followed by my eyes only healing part of the way since I was so weak and pathetic, barely worthy of being a werewolf at all. Hensley's Syndrome came through the male line, and it didn't affect alphas—it couldn't even be passed down by alphas as far as all the scientific literature said. So my father was a medical miracle, basically, only in the worst possible way.

And he insisted that had to be covered up at all costs to protect his own reputation as the perfect alpha, the perfect CEO. My reputation didn't matter, of course. Holding me up to ridicule instead didn't bother him at all.

Of course, my extended family and their friends thinking that story was laughable rather than tragic—an injured teenager who couldn't heal, damaged for life—was another fucking issue all on its own.

No one had ever questioned the lie. After all, everyone else in my family appeared to be perfect. Who'd suspect a genetic cause of my glaring flaws, right?

No one had questioned it until Pechorin, that is.

"What do you want? To keep your mouth shut."

He stared at me, his mouth, ironically, dropping open. "What?" he demanded. "You fucking—*what*?"

"To keep what you figured out to yourself," I gritted out. "How much money?"

His brows furrowed as he frowned down at me, eyes lighting with the faintest hint of an alpha glow.

"How can this be a secret?" he asked after a long pause. "How the fuck does everyone not know? You'd have to have seen doctors. Any kind of chronic health problem in a werewolf is weird. Noticeable."

"The doctors got paid off. Just like I'm offering to pay you. How much? I'll get the cash, you take it and walk away, and I never see or hear from you again."

The tight, heavy clench in the pit of my stomach owed about half to wondering how the hell I'd be able to afford what he'd be able to demand—more than he'd have asked for to mate me, I was sure—without asking my father, which would mean coming up with an explanation for this whole debacle.

The other half came from realizing it was over.

My plan had failed. And I truly was as pathetic as my family had always thought me.

Pechorin tilted his head, still frowning, examining me like an insect he'd found crawling on the floor. I felt like that, too: small and unwanted and ugly. Worthless.

"You made it sound like you'd be paying me a lot to mate with you. I agreed to that deal. I'm not trying to change it now. I'm not a fucking blackmailer, Castelli." Christ, he'd offered to kill Blake for money, unfunny joke or not. And now he had the nerve to sound insulted that I'd accused him of extortion? "I agree to do a job, I do that job. Not some other double-cross bullshit I come up with on the fly. I didn't research what was wrong with you to get money out of you. I did it because I like to know what I'm getting into."

"What you're getting into?" I asked faintly, stunned by his torrent of furious denial. He really, really did seem to be…wounded. Actually surprised that I'd suspected his intentions. "What the hell difference does it make to you? It's not like it's contagious. Or we're going to be reproducing."

Because we might actually still go through with this. Holy shit, he meant it. He meant to do it, because he'd said he would.

How long had it been since anyone had made a commitment to me and then followed through? Or even made a commitment in the first place?

"What happens if you have a seizure, huh? Or something else crops up. I'll be your mate. I'll be the one in charge of taking care of you. And if no one knows about this, and it's some kind of big secret I need to keep? That makes taking care of you—"

"I don't need anyone fucking taking care of me!" I snapped, pushing myself off the wall and right into his face, anger finally shaking me out of the haze of shock that'd fallen over me.

"The hell you don't!" he snapped back, leaning down so that mere inches separated our faces, alpha eyes blazing into mine. "You're a fucking mess, Castelli. Hiring someone like me to fuck and bite you proves that beyond the shadow of a doubt! And like I was saying—" I started to interject, and he had to raise his voice over my protests. "Like I was saying! The reason for us mating is a secret, obviously. Your medical condition: another secret. Something happens to you? I'm fucked, because I won't know how to handle it unless you tell me in advance. The secret comes out, or maybe you die because I don't know what to do. So yeah. This is something I needed to know. No more bullshit. I agreed to do this. I'm not going to take your money for nothing. But I'm not doing it unless you come clean. About everything so far, and anything else I don't already know."

The urge to obey him turned my thoughts and my blood sluggish, like poisoned honey. Fuck. That edge to his voice. No other alpha, including my father, had ever been able to affect me like this.

Obeying couldn't happen, because my father's secret, *our* secret…if it came out, everything would be ruined. There wouldn't be a company left for me to take over. And the board would never agree to having me in charge, anyway, not when I'd be seen as a liability too.

But he had a point; it couldn't be denied. Keeping the secret in general meant looping him in, and I'd been an idiot not to realize it. *I'm not going to take your money for nothing.* I kept coming back to that, too. It seemed like such a strange position for a man like Pechorin to take.

Maybe I'd misjudged him. Shit.

Even though, "You're a fucking mess, Castelli," also still rang in my ears. That made it a lot harder to feel bad about making assumptions.

"I have Hensley's," I said, forcing myself to put the words together slowly and carefully. "It's mostly my vision. I do have occasional seizures, but no grand mal so far. Myoclonic jerks—my legs start misbehaving, basically. Or I go a little fuzzy, but I don't pass out completely. Except for once, and that still was only a partial seizure. My doctor says I'm not at risk for any of the more serious symptoms."

Pechorin absorbed that for a moment, and then nodded.

"Fine," he said shortly. "But I'm not taking responsibility for it if something happens to you because you're in denial."

"I am *not* in denial!"

Which of course made me sound defensive. And in denial.

"Uh-huh."

"I'm not!"

Pechorin shrugged. "Whatever. Let's get down to business. As long as you're not hiding anything else I need to know."

I resisted putting a hand behind my back and crossing my

fingers. If he hadn't read deeply enough to learn that alphas shouldn't be able to carry Hensley's, or to connect the dots on which of my parents I must've inherited it from, I simply couldn't bring myself to be the one to enlighten him.

"I'm not."

He narrowed his eyes at me suspiciously, but then he shrugged again and turned away toward the table, pulling out one of the chairs and dropping into it.

For just a moment, I let myself lean my head back against the wall and take a breath, relieved of his looming, unsettling nearness.

And then I pushed off the wall, put on my game face, and joined him at the table.

If I wanted to run Castelli Industries, I had to be able to handle this.

Chapter 3

Big, Dumb, and Polite

Pechorin's price for mating me turned out to be a hundred thousand dollars. I choked a little. That would wipe out the money I'd been able to put aside from my monthly payments from my trust and from my salary. The lifestyle my family required me to lead—the expensive clothes and car and dinners and accoutrements—took most of my income. And I was also pretty sure I'd have paid that much *not* to take his knot, but here we were. That said…I still didn't have any better ideas.

"Jesus Christ, how much do you owe?" I had to ask, when he named the sum.

"Sixty grand," he said easily, without any hesitation. He'd leaned back in his chair, sprawled with one elbow propped on the armrest like a man without a care in the world. Only the faint golden glow in his eyes betrayed him. "But I borrowed the money for reasons that still stand. I need the other forty. And I won't do it for less. Plus a stipend if this mating lasts a while. We can discuss that."

"Reasons? Because I'm not going into this blind, either."

"Family issue. Not your business. Nothing that's going to bite you in the ass." He bared his teeth at me. "That's my job, apparently."

And oookay, not touching that one. My cheeks went hot and I shifted uncomfortably in my chair. Mating bites went on the neck, but my ass would be involved in other ways. Just the thought of his knot forcing me open had me squirming.

All right. Moving on. No point in dwelling on that.

Since I was still keeping some family secrets of my own even after making him believe otherwise, I didn't feel like pushing it on his "family issue," either. Which still left his other problems.

"And the packs after you? What happened there?"

Pechorin eyed my pen, which I'd started tapping against the

notepad open on the table in front of me. "You're not going to be writing this down, are you? And what is all that?"

Fuck. I slapped the notepad shut. "None of your beeswax. I'm not writing anything else down."

He gave me a slow, lazy grin that had all my hackles up in an instant.

Well, my remaining hackles. Most of them had been up since I walked into that bar.

"None of your beeswax," he repeated, grinning even wider. "You sound like my grandmother. Good thing you don't look like her, or we'd have a real problem regarding the mating part of this deal." As I sputtered, helpless to form an answer to that, he continued with, "And I can read upside down, especially when your handwriting's that obsessively neat. I was just being polite by asking. You were really hoping you could talk me into being the one to take your cock, huh? With bullet points and everything."

"I know you're not going to—I wasn't—" I fumbled frantically with the notepad and then yanked my hands back, forcing them into my lap. I'd already closed it. He might be able to read upside down, but he didn't have X-ray vision, for fuck's sake. Deep breaths. Close my eyes for a second. Christ. When I opened them again, Pechorin hadn't moved, staring at me with those intense eyes and the hint of a smile still playing over his lips. "I won't take any notes if you'd prefer I didn't, but it helps me organize my thoughts. And this mating's supposed to make me look good to the company's board, not worse. I need to know who's after you and why so we can deal with it."

His jaw tightened, and the remains of that smile evaporated. "I'll tell you what you want to know if you give me a straight answer on something else," he said. "Why me? I asked you yesterday. You didn't answer, except to tell me you weren't planning on trying to have me killed. You had more notes there," and he nodded at the pad of paper, "about how I need to behave. Dress. Present myself. I'm not what you're looking for. And I'm not crazy about being *My Fair Lady*, or whatever."

A sudden vision of Pechorin wearing one of those flower-feather-monstrosity hats Audrey Hepburn had on in the movie assailed me, and I choked on a laugh, coughing into my fist, eyes watering. "Sorry, sorry, fuck," I gasped, as he frowned at me, brows drawing together like a gathering thunderstorm. "Sorry," I said more soberly. "Look. I'm more attractive than Rex Harrison, at least, right?"

He stared at me blankly. "Who?"

Well, so much for lightening the mood with a little humor.

"The actor from *My Fair*—how do you know the movie without—okay, never mind, Christ. Pechorin, I don't give a fuck how you dress or behave when we're alone, but you need to fit the role in public for this to work. I'm trying to get the job of CEO. You'll need to look and act like the kind of man who'd be mated to one. An alpha who'd inspire confidence in a bunch of stuffy werewolf executives."

He leaned forward, resting his forearms on the table and fixing me with an intense, penetrating gaze. That bastard, using my own practiced strong-negotiator posture on me! But something lurked in the depths of those eyes that made me...ashamed, of all things. Something that could see all the way to the cowardly, jealous, bitter person I was deep down.

I hated feeling like that.

"What?" I snapped. "It's a perfectly reasonable requirement. This is what I need. And I'm guessing you're wondering why I'd pick you when I could find a different alpha with the right background without too much trouble?"

He nodded.

The way he watched me, so quietly unyielding in his determination to get me to explain myself, made my fingers twitch with the urge to fidget. I couldn't quite meet his eyes.

"Someone like that, with the pedigree my family would want, would take over for real. Push me out. He'd get promoted in my place. No one's going to expect or want you to become the CEO, because aside from the knot, you don't have any qualifications. You just need to be polished enough that we won't be a laughingstock. You're supposed to prop me up, remember? That's the whole point."

After a beat, he said, "Sure, I guess it is." Pechorin leaned back again, in the same position he'd occupied before—but with tension in the set of his shoulders and in his massive frame. "So. Spiffed up but not competition. That's what you're looking for? Wear a suit, but not as well as you do. Don't get in any fights, but growl when necessary. Big, dumb, and polite. That about it?"

Agreeing with him felt more insulting than I could justify. The irony, of course, being that he was far from dumb. And trying to sugarcoat the truth—that yes, I wanted big, dumb, and polite, with a limited amount of growling available as necessary—would only be condescending. And hence even more insulting.

Oddly, I realized I wasn't worried that he'd hurt me if I pissed him off. Not anymore. That had clearly been an error in judgment too, even if it'd been a rational error to make. I'd spent enough time around alphas to know when violence might be imminent, and except for my moment of paranoia the night before in the parking lot, he hadn't set off any alarm bells in that regard.

I just didn't want to insult him. We'd be mated.

Jesus fucking Christ, we'd be *mated*, and whatever tone we set now would be what I'd have to live with in private for who knew how long. Months, at least. Maybe years.

But I'd hesitated too long, losing my chance either to be honest or to be tactful, or hopefully even both.

Pechorin's mouth quirked in a humorless half smile. "Yeah, that's what I thought."

Shit. "Look, Pechorin—"

"Might want to get used to calling me Dimitri, *Brook*. If you're planning to convince all your snobby relatives that you mated me because you fell in love, or something. I guess you could fall back on telling them you're with me for my knot. Maybe they'd believe that. After all, that seems to be all they care about, so why wouldn't you?"

Yeah. Yeah, they probably would believe that, since they thought any guy who took a knot was weak, and they thought I was weak, so connect the dots. They'd held out hope for a while that maybe I'd mate with a woman and produce some alpha offspring, be useful by proxy, but I had no intention of risking passing on Hensley's to any non-alpha children—and now that they'd finally accepted that women weren't my thing, they'd pivoted to trying to push an alpha on me.

But taking a knot wasn't my thing, either. I enjoyed topping, dammit. I hadn't been lying when I told Pechorin that.

Fuck. Not Pechorin; Dimitri.

"Yeah, maybe they would," I said, my voice rasping in my throat. So I probably deserved his sarcasm-bordering-on-mockery, but that didn't make it any more pleasant. Less, actually. "And you're right. We need to get more comfortable with each other, or at least act like it. Dimitri. Am I pronouncing it right?"

His eyes flared with alpha gold for a second, and he shifted in his chair. "Close enough," he said, as roughly as I'd spoken myself.

Had it made him angry, hearing me use his first name? Since I had the feeling he didn't like me much? I wasn't going to ask, especially since it'd been his damn idea. My name on his lips had given me an odd little shiver, as if the intimacy of it heralded further, less welcome, intimacy to come. Maybe he'd had the same issue. Knotting me couldn't possibly be worse from his side of the equation, could it? I knew I'd be overjoyed if I were on the other side of this instead of knowing that every second brought me closer to bending over for this harsh, sardonic alpha I didn't know and had to force myself to trust.

"I'll try to get better with the pronunciation," I replied at last, flailing for something, anything to say. "Sound more natural."

He shrugged. "No one but me's going to know the difference. I doubt it matters that much."

A heavy silence fell.

I broke it with, "I still need to know what trouble you're in, Dimitri. Who's going to come calling? Do they need to be paid off too? And don't try to leave anything out, please. I looked into your antecedents. I know you have at least three packs on your tail, figuratively if not literally."

For a moment I thought he wouldn't answer me at all—and my lame werewolf joke didn't even get me a smile, dammit. Finally he sighed, ran a hand over the lower half of his face, and started to talk.

My eyes got wider as he did, even though perhaps for someone like Dimitri the story wasn't all that shocking. I hadn't thought I'd been particularly sheltered, but apparently I'd been wrong. The first pack, he assured me, wouldn't be a problem. He'd gotten in a fight with the pack enforcers and they'd taken issue with the fact that

Dimitri won. "They were after me for a while. But the asshole in charge got himself killed in California a while back," he added dismissively. "So I doubt they're going to give a shit about me anymore. Too busy killing each other to try to fill the vacuum."

Before I could do more than stare and try to process this, he moved on to the second: a pack in Montana. "That one's more of a 'I fucked the pack leader's mate' kind of issue, and once I mate into a powerful pack he'll drop it. The third—"

"An 'I fucked the pack leader's mate kind of thing'? Are you insane?"

Dimitri stopped and blinked at me. "She was really hot. Anyway, they broke their bond and he mated someone else. No harm, no foul."

"No harm," I choked out, and ran my hands through my hair as if that could somehow soothe my aching brain. "No foul. Right. Christ. Dimitri, do you just stir up trouble wherever you go?"

His eyes narrowed. "I'm not going to stir up any trouble for you or in your pack," he said, picking up on my implied concerns about our deal without missing a beat. How could someone so obviously intelligent also act like such an idiot so often? "I'm not that much of a loose cannon, actually. I just usually don't care. This time, I do. It's too much money on the table not to care. Anyway, the third pack's the only one that could be an issue, because we had some financial dealings that went south. But if they do track me down, paying them off will take care of it. They're practical guys and not looking for an unnecessary fight. If you want to add an extra twelve grand to the deal, I'll send them the money before they come calling and get rid of the problem."

My jaw tensed until my teeth pressed together. I unclenched enough to speak with a conscious effort. "You could always pay them out of the forty thousand you'll already have to spare."

"It's not to spare." Dimitri didn't look away, didn't change expression in the slightest. Uncompromising. "If you want to make sure my past associates don't show up to embarrass you, that's how much it'll cost you. I wasn't going to bother asking for it, because I'm not all that worried about it. Not now that I'll have a safe haven and some backup. They won't want to take on the Castelli pack."

The extra twelve thousand rankled. I could afford it, but a hundred and twelve thousand dollars, plus that possible stipend…Dimitri couldn't possibly be worth that.

"Pay them out of what I'm already giving you. Or no deal. I don't want them showing up and fucking up my plans, and I'm not giving you any more than we already agreed to."

I stared him down without flinching, even though the set of his shoulders and the faint golden glow illuminating those hard gray irises made me want to duck my head and curl in on myself. Damn it, he wasn't the only one who could be uncompromising. Compromise shouldn't always be the job of the not-alpha in the room. I spent enough time living like that already without my fake mate putting me in the same position.

"Fine," he said at last, a single, clipped syllable without any emotion behind it at all.

"Good." I nodded and wished I'd left my notepad open so that I could close it briskly in emphasis. That always had the desired effect in meetings at work. "We're agreed. We'll need to take you shopping, get you ready to meet my fam—"

He leaned forward, a grim smile lifting the corners of his mouth. "Pretty sure we'll need to fuck first, yeah? And there's a bed right there."

My eyes flicked to the left without my volition. There was indeed a bed. Right there. Ugly bedspread and all. I could not possibly get knotted for the first—and, I promised myself, only—time on something made out of shiny polyester.

A shudder went down my spine. Ugh.

"We get ourselves organized first. Clothes, a few pointers on how to act. Then we mate and I put your name on a bank account with a hundred grand in it. We can do that the same day, so we're both comfortable with it. And then we break the news to my family. Deal?"

Dimitri considered me for a moment, glanced over at the bed, and grimaced. Well, how fucking flattering. Not that I didn't agree with him, but still.

"How long is it going to take to 'get organized'? I need the money."

"A couple of days, if you're a quick study." I was willing to bet he would be. He'd figured out the Hensley's thing fast enough. Big he might be, but dumb and polite were a stretch.

"Fine. Then we have a deal." He stuck out his hand across the table.

Gingerly, I reached out and took it. His alpha-hot fingers enveloped mine, long and strong and rough. The heat of him lanced up my arm and lodged somewhere under my sternum, nearly taking my breath away. Unlike every other alpha I'd shaken hands with, he didn't try to crush my hand or show his strength; he just shook like a normal guy, a firm pressure and then release. When he let me go, his touch lingered, like a brand.

Chapter 4

You're Stalling

We didn't have a snappy soundtrack, and Dimitri didn't demand that any store clerks give me their ties, but otherwise our day out shopping reminded me powerfully of *Pretty Woman*. Desperate, weirdo rich guy paying for someone way more objectively attractive to pretend to date him: check. Simmering awkwardness between the protagonists: check. Sidelong looks from everyone who helped us in the stores: very much check, because we made a suspicious pair, me dressed in clothes ten times more expensive than the ones I was buying for him with a no-limit credit card, and him glowering at ties like he expected them to leap up and try to strangle him.

We even got pizza despite my objections to the plastic-like cheese and not-organic sauce—although we carried it ourselves to a small, grimy table in the mall food court, rather than having it delivered by a flunky.

We already had a pile of bags around us, and Dimitri had rebelled at the idea of trying on "one more fucking monkey suit" before he got fed.

I paid, obviously. And I'd rather have paid another several hundred dollars for another suit than the five bucks it cost to be fed cardboard with subpar tomato stuff on it.

The ambiance didn't help. Skylights in the high ceiling let in enough sun, glaring down and reflecting off of all the white plastic tables and beams, to make the huge, echoing food court hot and far too bright for a normal person, let alone someone with my weak, sensitive eyes. Mingled odors of MSG-laden fake-Chinese and reheated greasy burgers made my stomach churn.

Dimitri had already wolfed down three slices, pun fully intended, before I'd done more than nibble the end of my one.

"You could've gotten something else," he groused around

another monstrous bite. Table manners. That would be lesson number one. "There's like ten places to eat here. Or do you live on gold-plated caviar or something?"

He leaned over and polished off his fourth slice of pizza, totally unconcerned by my scowl.

"For one thing, I don't even like fish, fish products, or anything fish-related. For two, ha fucking ha. I'm not a snob. I'm just not that hungry."

"Okay." He dropped a fragment of burned crust on his paper plate. "You going to eat that, or not?"

I pushed my own plate across the table without a word, and he dug in.

My phone buzzed in my pocket, and I pulled it out: Yet another email from my assistant, who'd been left to hold down the fort while I took Friday off. Jackie seemed to think I must be dying if I hadn't come to the office. On the other hand, she hadn't stopped sending me questions, either. A presentation that I hadn't signed off on. Spreadsheets not adding up. The legal department had an HR issue that someone had punted to me for some unknown, ungodly reason. Death, apparently, was no excuse for avoiding the HR team. My temples throbbed.

And apparently Blake had been looking for me.

Well, that did it. In a burst of furious rebellion, I powered my phone *actually all the way off* and stuck it back in my pocket.

When I glanced up again, Dimitri had finished the last crumb of my erstwhile lunch and was eyeing me in a way I didn't like. That look seemed to flash right through me like an X-ray, and I could feel my cheeks heating up.

"What?" I snapped.

"You might as well have jumped up on the table and started shouting 'Give me freedom or give me death.' When's the last time you turned that fucking thing off? Ever? And you're off work today. The fuck are you doing checking it in the first place?"

I'd never turned it off, in fact. And I'd taken a "day off" three years ago, approximately, when my cousin got married. I'd missed most of the ceremony taking a call from a panicked client with a software glitch. Since said glitch could've, worst-case scenario, caused a dam to release millions of gallons of water and flood a whole valley, it'd seemed worth it to step out.

That cousin kind of sucked anyway—and she'd already gotten divorced, so it wasn't like I'd missed much.

My father had still been pissed about my breach of etiquette, even though he would've taken the call too. He'd have been doubly pissed if I'd sent it to voicemail.

Blake had been the best man.

I simply couldn't win.

"You know, you get that sucking-a-rotten-lemon look on your face every time you're thinking about work," Dimitri commented, breaking me out of my brooding. "Maybe you should quit. Ditch the job, your shitty family, all of it. Go do your own thing."

The grain—okay, fine, metric ton—of truth in that infuriated me, my heart pounding and my fists clenching. How dare he be right! Especially when fear of the unknown and of being alone was mostly what was stopping me. Asshole.

"You don't know my family, and you don't have any right to comment on them," I growled, my own werewolf nature surging to the surface. My fingertips itched, claws aching to come out. "And if I did that, you could say goodbye to your easy payday. So maybe you should shut the fuck up."

"Okay," Dimitri said, his tone so low and even it raised the hairs on the back of my neck. Shouldn't he have been snapping in turn? But he'd sat back in his uncomfortable molded plastic chair, reclining as if it actually fit his massive frame. Were his eyes glowing? Given the glare from the skylights and my poor eyesight, I couldn't tell. "Big, dumb, polite, and also silent. Got it. Wear the suits, look alpha, and shut the fuck up."

A little bit of guilt crept in around the edges of my temper. My family—and they were in fact shitty, just like he'd said—weren't his fault. And neither was anything else that'd happened to me before we'd met, for that matter.

"I didn't mean it like—"

"I said I got it." This time his tone had some bite to it, and it stopped me in my verbal tracks. "I've made worse deals. That's why I'm on everyone's shit list and in so much debt, right? So forget it.

I'll keep my mouth shut and my opinions to myself."

I had to try one more time, even though the tight, heavy lump in my gut made me want to curl in on myself and hide. "You're welcome to express—"

"No." That single syllable hit me like a blow to the already-aching stomach, hard and filled with contempt. "What's next? We have enough clothes. We should get going."

That totally false statement distracted me from everything else. *Enough clothes?* Was he *nuts?*

"We have suits and a couple of shirts, but you need more. And then there's jeans, slacks, belts, shoes, and accessor—"

"You're—"

The third time was seriously not the charm, something I was rapidly beginning to think he didn't have any of. "Stop interrupting me! So far you're not doing a very good job of being polite *or* silent!"

"Then stop talking like an asshole!"

Dimitri lunged forward across the table, snarling at me, and I realized I'd leaned forward too. Our faces were only inches apart. Aside from the alpha gold now *definitely* overlaying his eyes, the gray of his irises held gleaming flecks of mossy green, and dark blue ringed the outside. Jesus Christ, those were nice eyes. The kind you could look at for a long time before you got tired of—I flung myself back into my seat like a snake had bitten my nose.

Oh, fucking hell. I panted for breath, way too worked up for someone who'd just been gazing into Dimitri Pechorin's eyes.

He didn't move, still fixing me with that hard, penetrating stare, lips curled to show me a hint of fang. And I couldn't have moved if I'd been the one getting paid a hundred grand, pinned there with all my muscles locked up.

"You're stalling," he said at last, slowly, as if working his way through a chain of logic. "How much of a wardrobe do I really need before we even get down to business? I only need to look respectable for a first meet and greet with your family. What's next, a series of etiquette lessons? Do you even want to go through with this? Or are you wasting my fucking time?"

Since I'd been considering etiquette lessons a few minutes before while watching him eat, only my state of frozen immobility prevented a visible flinch.

"It's my time too. And my dime," I managed.

"Not yet," he shot back. "Since you haven't paid me a fucking cent."

"I've bought you all this—"

He bulldozed right over my protest. "All this shit I don't want or need, yeah. You've spent a lot of money on stalling, I'll give you that." Dimitri laid his hands flat on the table, fingers flexing slightly as if he was trying to keep his own claws in. Christ, that would be perfect: my criminal alpha Eliza Doolittle wolfing out in a mall food court and causing a riot. "No more bullshit. We get all this crap loaded up in the car and go from here to the bank. You give me the money. And then we go to your place, or wherever else you want to do this, and we mate. Today. Final offer, Brook. Do it or don't."

Fuck. Today. Right now. My mouth went dry, my head spinning. He wasn't ready. My family wouldn't accept him, and it'd all be for nothing.

There had to be some way to put this off.

But there really wasn't, because the firm set of Dimitri's jaw and the hard, uncompromising glint in his alpha-glowing eyes told me I'd run out of room for negotiation.

"There is no try," I mumbled, like a moron.

Dimitri went still, staring at me like I'd started speaking in tongues. Jesus, a guy wasn't allowed to make a *Star Wars* reference, or something?

"Huh," he said at last, cryptically. "So? What's the verdict? I can go either way on this. But if you want my opinion—" He cut himself off, shaking his head. "Right. No more opinions. What are we doing?"

That falling-off-the-cliff feeling I'd had when I agreed to meet him in the hotel room came rushing back, heady and terrifying. Would he be there to catch me when I hit the ground? I'd be handing him so much power over me: he'd be able to physically dominate me in my own space, control my shift if he felt inclined, use his alpha power and his status as the dominant mate to enforce any behavior he wanted. At least I knew he wouldn't be abusing his alpha strength to use me sexually, since he didn't want to fuck me in the first place.

A deep breath, shaky and not quite hitting the bottoms of my lungs, didn't do much to settle me.

"We're going to the bank. And then—and then we're going to my house." Maybe the gate guard would tell my mother I'd brought home a guest. But she'd be going out of town this weekend for a spa getaway, and by the time she asked me about it, I'd already be introducing Dimitri as my mate. Besides, I couldn't face doing what I had to do anywhere but in my own safe den, surrounded by the sight and scent of my own possessions and space. "We can mate there."

Dimitri let out a long, slow exhale, something like relief flitting across his harsh face.

"Then let's go. I can carry the bags. That seems like a job for someone big, dumb, and polite, right?" He stood up, suiting the action to the words, gathering up all of the shopping in his big, rough hands.

It should've made him look ridiculous, a bulky, broad-shouldered guy like that with his resting-murderer-face holding all those gaudy, shiny bags with tissue poking out the tops.

Instead, it made me *feel* ridiculous for having bought it all in the first place.

"Silent. You forgot silent," I snapped, getting out of my own chair with none of Dimitri's predatory grace. Stress made my condition worse, and I could only pray I didn't start having any seizure activity on top of the clumsiness and lack of balance.

Dimitri grunted. "Don't take your bad mood out on me, princess. This wasn't my idea. I'm just along for the ride." He flashed his fangs at me. "And the money."

Princess? What a fucking asshole. "Don't call me that. It's demeaning."

I did my best to sweep past him with my nose in the air, but I ended up bonking my hip on the edge of the table and skittering past him cursing under my breath instead.

"What's demeaning about it?" he rumbled from behind me, as I weaved my way through the scattered tables and chairs, trying not to trip over other people's shopping on my way out of the food court. "You're rich, pretty, and snobby, and you're looking for a husband to rescue you from your shitty family. The shoe fits, so to speak."

Okay, fine, nice fairy tale pun there, but the rest of it…pretty? No one had ever called me that before.

I wasn't, obviously. And that was even more demeaning. The righteous anger I tried to dredge up wouldn't quite materialize, though.

"You're Cinderella in this scenario, *princess*. If I'm the rich one. You're the one with the bags full of new clothes."

I finally cleared the last row of trash cans and made it into the more open space of the mall proper, and Dimitri fell into step beside me. A glance up at him showed me a crooked grin and gleaming eyes.

"That makes you the fairy godmother, actually. Maybe you should drop this analogy while you're only a little bit behind."

My face burning, I opened my mouth to let out any one, or maybe several, of the scathing retorts that popped into my head. But then I turned, meaning to look him in the eyes while I told him what I thought of him.

And the urge to continue arguing withered away. His smile looked genuine. Amused, and not necessarily at my expense, either. Like he'd been enjoying bantering with me rather than using it as a way to put me down, as I'd assumed.

He'd had me on the defensive since I first walked into that bar and saw him there waiting for me. Maybe I'd been on the defensive before I even met him, expecting the same kind of contempt and dismissal I received from my family and many of my colleagues on a daily basis. Alphas looked down on me; that was the way of the world.

Maybe I needed to get out more.

I stopped in my tracks, Dimitri coming to a halt beside me, and cocked my head and examined him, trying to see him objectively rather than through the lens of insecurity and anxiety and fear.

"What?" he demanded. "Do I have something on my face?"

He'd had that honestly pretty nice smile on his face, until me staring at him weirdly had wiped it away.

We could be allies, rather than unwilling, adversarial co-conspirators. And maybe all I had to do to bring that about was…stop being adversarial.

Jesus. Could it possibly be that easy? Just trust him? Try to relax a little for once?

This time, when I sucked in as much oxygen as I could hold, my lungs filled all the way, and the tension flowed in waves all the way down to my toes, down and out.

"Are you really going to help me?" I asked, trying not to sound pitiful and needy, but…yeah, not really succeeding. My voice had a plaintive note to it that took my blush to surface-of-the-sun levels. "I mean, you're going to do your best, right? Good-faith effort?"

The furrow between Dimitri's brows smoothed out somewhat, and that smile came back. Not all the way, but a hint of it at the corners of his mouth and in the softened light in his gray eyes.

"I'd like to," he said, a lot more gently than I expected. Or possibly deserved. "I already told you, if I'm paid to do a job, I do the job. Period."

Trust. It had to be a leap of faith, right? Maybe he *would* catch me when I fell. And I'd never know if I didn't give him the opportunity to prove it.

I smiled up at him in return, my facial muscles protesting. Yeah, I could probably stand to smile a little more in general.

"The pack has a shaman. Maybe I can get him to enchant some lizards, or something. If that'd give you a better Cinderella experience. I'm afraid that's outside of my capabilities, but part of management is delegation, right?"

Dimitri's full-throated, head-thrown-back laugh hit me like a flash grenade, leaving me blinking and rocking back on my heels. How could a man like this have a laugh like *that?* Warm and deep and infectious, making my sad attempt at a smile widen into something real.

He grinned down at me, eyes bright. "I'll give the enchanted lizards a pass, thanks. But look, if I'm Cinderella, you're right. I need one pair of new shoes to go with the suits. One pair of shoes, one belt, and then we're out of this fucking mall before I crawl out of my own skin. Deal?"

Well, that was a meeting-me-halfway peace offering if ever I'd heard one. More than halfway, even. A genuine concession.

"One pair of shoes, one belt. And we can go to the department store that's on the way out to the car." It gave me almost physical pain to suggest that, rather than insisting on backtracking to the much preferable upscale haberdashery at the other end of the mall, but when Dimitri nodded in obvious relief, his smile sticking around…worth it.

"I won't argue, even if they look dumb," Dimitri said.

I shoved down the brief flare of annoyance. Dumb? Good taste was never dumb. But he was trying, dammit.

When we turned and set off for the store, the atmosphere between us was practically friendly.

Chapter 5

Point of View

My sense of ease had drained away completely by the time I unlocked the front door of my house and awkwardly ushered Dimitri inside.

"So. This is home," I said, pushing the door shut behind him with an echoing click.

Or maybe it only echoed in my throbbing head.

Dimitri dropped the bags and glanced around the foyer before shrugging and taking off into the house without even being invited.

Well, the hundred thousand dollars I'd just transferred to him so that he'd be willing to fuck me probably qualified as an invitation, to be fair.

"This is McMansion hell." His voice drifted back to me from somewhere deeper in the house. "Is there some reason why everything's all kind of tan-colored?"

The short and truthful answer: my mother thought beige was "classy," and I didn't have a spine.

The answer I gave, once I'd swallowed down my rising irritation: "It's neutral and you don't need to worry about it not matching anything." I followed him out of the foyer and down a few steps into the large sunken living room, with its enormous sectional camel-colored sofa, an area rug in various shades of oatmeal, a variety of coordinating lamps and end tables, and a few painfully bland abstract paintings on the walls. "It's not so bad." It was so, so bad. "Besides, I'm hardly ever here, as in this room or most of the downstairs, period. If I'm not at work, I'm in my home office or my bedroom."

Dimitri turned around from where he'd been twitching aside the (beige) blinds to peer out the front window and frowned at me. "It's like you go out of your way to make your life as fucking depressing as possible."

There went the last of my Zen.

"It's just a house," I snapped. "Not some commentary on my mental state."

He grimaced, raised his eyebrows, and then mimed zipping his lips shut.

I stared at him for a moment, contemplating the life choices that had led me to need to pay this man to fuck me up the ass and bite me on the neck.

Depressing barely even began to cover it.

"So are we going to do this mating thing or not? I'm a hundred grand richer, so I'm ready to go. And it's not like we're going to enjoy it more for putting it off, right?"

That stung a lot more than I wanted to admit. Alphas were notorious for sticking their dicks in anyone who'd hold still long enough. Hadn't he called me *pretty*? Maybe that had been an insult after all.

"Didn't you zip your mouth literally two seconds ago?"

Another shrug. "I'm not saying anything else about your furniture, am I? So where's your bedroom? Unless you'd rather get knotted over the back of that couch, in which case we should maybe talk a little more about your relationship with the décor in here."

I had to consciously relax my jaw to answer. "Ha fucking ha," was the best response I could muster.

Get knotted.

That was going to happen to me.

Right now.

Christ, my ass muscles were clenching as hard as my teeth.

"I'm going to go take a shower. Make yourself at home," I added, realizing with a pang that whether or not I meant it, he would be doing exactly that. Since he'd be moving in with me. At this moment, basically. Shit. "Actually, come on, let me give you a quick tour and then we can meet up in my bedroom. There's a guest room across the hall you can have. It has its own bathroom, so you'll have some privacy."

I turned for the stairs, and Dimitri followed me, his footsteps sounding heavily on the wood floor. "I'll take that as a hint to get in the shower myself while you're getting ready. Towels and stuff in there already?"

"Yeah." Oh my God, this was so agonizingly awkward. "That's my room, and that's your room now, I guess. And that's my office at the end of the hall. Um, everything's in there already. Like I already said. You can tell me if there's anything you need." Every word out of my mouth felt heavy, stilted, unnatural. I turned and found him a couple of inches behind me, looming and muscular and intimidating and about to *fuck me in the ass*, and I jumped and practically fell into the opposite wall. "Yeah. I'll be done soon."

And with that, I fled into my own bedroom and shut the door behind me a little too forcefully.

Shit, shit, shit.

"That wasn't me slamming it!" I called through the door. "Accident!"

My fingers had started to tingle again, and I squeezed my eyes shut as if that could make me disappear.

"Okay," Dimitri called back after a moment, sounding more confused than anything. "Roger that."

Christ, I was such a spaz.

A second later I heard his door shut, and I took a few deep breaths. Alone. I had some time alone, and I could get it together. When my eyes opened, I had to blink to try to clear the blurriness, but maybe my heart rate had gone down a tiny bit?

Undressing and showering took a lot longer than it should have, what with my clumsy fingers fumbling all my buttons, and the way I tripped trying to get out of my pants, and then my incredible reluctance to touch myself the way I needed to in order to wash in all the right places.

But at last, lightheaded from too long under too-hot water, presumably clean enough, and with my heart still thumping away, I shut off the shower and wrapped a towel around my waist, wiping a hand over the mirror so I could get a look at what Dimitri would be seeing when he came into my bedroom in a minute.

I wasn't impressed, and I doubted he would be either. Without my glasses on—and I wouldn't be wearing my glasses during sex, Jesus, I wasn't quite that much of a nerd—I had a slightly pinched look around the eyes, and divots in the bridge of my nose. Nice shoulders, though. Broad for my height.

Which would be a bug, not a feature, for a guy who had no interest in men.

Fuck it. A quick brush of my teeth, even though we wouldn't be kissing, and then I ditched the towel, headed into my bedroom, and hesitated. Under the covers? Would he laugh at me for being a prude? Face down, ass up? That had the advantage of being no-nonsense.

I compromised by getting out some lube and setting it on the nightstand, and then folding down the blanket and bedspread and sliding under the sheet, pulling that up to my waist.

The house lay in silence; Dimitri had probably finished with his own shower. My hearing, at least, was as good as the average werewolf's. "Dimitri? I'm ready," I said, knowing that his alpha ears would probably pick it up even if I whispered.

A second later the door across the hall opened followed by heavy footsteps, and then my own door opened.

Dimitri had gone for a T-shirt and boxers, both black, and the sight of him framed in my doorway took away what little breath I had left.

Jesus, he was big. From his broad shoulders and bulging biceps down to his tree-trunk legs and giant Yeti feet, he had all the proportions you'd expect of an alpha, and then some.

I couldn't help my eyes flicking down to the front of his boxers. Even soft, that visible bulge, visible even without my glasses on…I swallowed hard, another wave of dizziness hitting me. I'd gotten fucked exactly twice, when I was a junior in college and thought I ought to give it a fair shot. While it hadn't hurt, or anything traumatic like that, it hadn't been good. Just mechanical. A thing moving in and out of me. The guy I'd been seeing had gone way out of his way to be gentle, careful, checking in with me every two seconds to make sure he hadn't made me uncomfortable.

His constant concern had made me *so* fucking uncomfortable. I hadn't relaxed for even a moment.

"So, um. I'm ready," I said, when the silence had stretched to the breaking point, Dimitri not moving a muscle.

Finally he took a step into the room, shutting the door behind him. "You already use that?" He jerked his chin toward…the lube, right.

Dammit, what had I been thinking? He wouldn't want to finger me. *I* wouldn't want him to finger me, either, obviously.

"No. I mean, sorry. I should have. I guess that's what you thought I meant by 'ready,' right?"

He took another step, and then another, ratcheting up my tension foot by foot.

"Go ahead," he said, his voice gone deeper. "But I don't mind doing it if you'd rather. I have a better angle. You know, point of view."

I snatched the lube off the nightstand so quickly I nearly sprained my arm. *Point of view?* The only thing worse than watching Dimitri finger me open for his no-doubt massive cock would be watching him watch his fingers working inside my body.

Although once I got the bottle open and reached under the sheet, twisting my wrist at an intensely unergonomic angle, watching him watch me attempt to work my fingers inside my body turned out to be even worse. I got all flushed and sweaty, trying to keep from wincing as I pushed a finger in, the smoothness of my own flesh all weird and wrong—it felt like something I might want to fuck, and that gave me the heebie-jeebies. Not to mention it didn't feel good, and I didn't want it, and—

"Pull the sheet off and give me the lube, for fuck's sake," Dimitri said, and strode forward the last few feet, reaching for the sheet as he did.

"Wait! Hang on, I can—eep!"

I flailed as he whipped the sheet off of me, baring me to his dark, intent gaze. I had my knees up and a finger in me, and I pulled it out too quickly, the sting of it making me wince after all, and scuttled backward like a crab caught in an extremely compromising position.

Something in my expression of horror must have told him I was more than simply embarrassed, because he backed off a step, raising his hands in front of him.

"Hey," he said, low and calm. Like he was talking to a spooked animal. "Hey. It's okay. We have to do this, but I know you don't really want to. I'd like to help."

My whole body vibrated with the force of my galloping heart-beat, and my vision had gone blurry again. Two hazy Dimitris stood in front of me, both of them not. Helping. At all.

The tension in my legs had me nearly paralyzed…and then I realized they *were* paralyzed, so stiff I couldn't move them at all. My arm gave a little jerk, snapping away from my body.

Reality faded out completely, and my last thought was, *Oh, shit.*

***

Five years before, I'd had my one and only seizure involving impaired awareness. Usually, my seizures were tonic-clonic and I stayed awake the whole time. My muscles would stiffen and jerk, and I might start laughing, or not be able to speak.

But I stayed awake.

That episode five years ago had been right before I graduated with my master's degree. I'd barely been sleeping, my thesis still lacked fifteen pages and a coherent conclusion, I'd had too much to drink, and I'd gotten off the phone with my father, who'd told me he'd be giving my commencement a pass because some family friend or other had invited him and Blake golfing for the weekend.

I never knew how long it lasted; probably not more than a mi-nute or two. But it felt like hours had passed when I came around, sprawled on the floor next to the couch in my student apartment, my mouth cottony with carpet dust. I didn't have any injuries, which wasn't too surprising given my neurologist's predictions about the types of seizures I'd be prone to. I'd just collapsed and stayed there without moving around.

But the mental fog, the complete inability to figure out where the hell I was and what was going on, had been worse than bruises or a bitten tongue would've been.

That and the crippling terror. It felt like I was dying, and it took an endless, agonizing minute, maybe, for that to fade and for some-thing approximating reality and understanding of what had happened to set in.

This time wasn't all that different at first.

Lying down, having trouble breathing, my body a throbbing mess of awfulness. Dry mouth. Thoughts moving like molasses, slow and dark and oozing through my mental fingers when I tried to grab onto them.

And the fear. The fear that I'd die like this, that…and then I remembered the last time, the memory seeping in through a crack in my confusion.

Not dying. Had a seizure. It didn't help the chaos in my brain, but at least I didn't need to panic.

Physical sensations came back while I waited for my brain and my mouth to reboot. I'd been so cold and aching and lonely in a deeply visceral way last time, desperate for the anchor of another living being.

But not this time. This part was different.

To a werewolf raised in a properly loving family and pack, the scent of an alpha meant safety, protection, all being right with the world. The knowledge that whatever had gone wrong, someone was in the process of fixing it. Friends of mine who'd had that kind of upbringing had told me all about it, and it'd made sense to me on a bone-deep, instinctual level, deep in the part of me that *wanted*. But I'd also found it hard to relate to. Alpha scents and the similar, but much more subtle, feeling of their enhanced shifter magic wrapping around me set me on edge. It meant my father. It meant Blake. It meant criticism and scorn and bracing myself for another figurative blow.

For the first time in my life, I scented and sensed an alpha without freezing up, going on the defensive.

Warm and fresh all at once, like the hint of a cool sea breeze tendriling through the heat of a summer's day. This alpha had a little dash of citrus in his scent, grapefruit maybe. And something else, something darker and sharper and hot like a spark off of steel.

His magic enclosed and sheltered me. Strength radiated from him, absorbing into my chilled, stiff muscles.

Getting my eyes open took some serious effort. I didn't know who was there, only that maybe I'd figure it out if I could see him.

After a few blinks, a harsh-featured man with messy dark hair and beautiful eyes wavered into focus. I knew his name. I *knew* I knew his name. But it wouldn't quite come. So frustrating. My head fit perfectly tucked onto his shoulder, and his arm around my ribs felt strong enough to hold me forever. He lay next to me on my bed, on his side with the rest of his body held a respectable distance away. He wasn't crowding me, and I kind of wished he would.

"Do you know where you are?" His voice matched his scent and feel and heat, all dark and rumbly and soothing. "Can you tell me what day of the week it is?"

I did know where I was: home, in my own bed. The seizure must've happened here, unless he'd moved me to make me more comfortable. The words wouldn't come, though. I managed to nod. The day of the week? My lips moved, trying to tell him I wasn't quite sure but I knew it was a weekday, and my brain wasn't broken, just...temporarily stalled out. No sound emerged.

"Huh," he said. "I read online that you're supposed to ask questions like that after someone has a seizure. But I also read that some seizures make you unable to talk. So it seems kind of dumb to me." He shrugged, my head rising and falling with the gesture. "Whatever. We'll wait a little bit. If you still can't talk, and you're confused, then we'll figure out where to go from there. Your pack must have a doctor or a shaman or someone who's in the know about the Hensley's thing."

A quick, sharp spike of panic lanced through me. Why the hell was *he* in the know about the Hensley's thing? I wasn't supposed to tell anyone. I couldn't tell anyone, because...Dimitri. This was Dimitri, and the relief of remembering canceled out the anxiety about him knowing my secret. More came back with the name, though: the mating plan, the shopping trip, coming home.

Having a seizure while trying to finger my ass open to let him fuck me.

I squeezed my eyes shut, and I'd have been shaking with humiliation if I'd had the energy. That weird sound...yeah, that was me, some kind of groan/whimper hybrid that totally failed to express my true feelings.

"Don't," Dimitri said. "See, this is why I needed to know this could happen. I read up on it so I could be prepared. There's nothing to be upset about."

Nothing to be upset about? He wasn't the one in the midst of suffering the most agonizing embarrassment of his life!

"Brook. Look at me." Dimitri didn't say it unkindly, but I could've gotten up and danced a jig sooner than ignore the alpha command in his voice.

When I fluttered my eyes open, he'd leaned down over me, his face close enough for me to make out every detail. God, he had such nice eyes, even with the furrow of a frown between them. Those little bits of green were so damn pretty.

Pretty didn't seem like quite the right word to describe Dimitri, though. More like the opposite.

He'd called me pretty. Bet he didn't think that now.

A fresh wave of total humiliation rolled over me and washed me under.

"There really isn't." It took me a second to realize he was continuing the thread of what he'd been saying before. And I still disagreed, strongly. "Brook, I've had sex before. A lot of sex. Super fucking awkward sex, like the time my date to my high school prom threw up while she was trying to give me a blowjob."

Laughter rose up and choked me, my diaphragm spasming. My head spun, and then spun some more as Dimitri lifted me effortlessly with the arm underneath me, pulling me up to lean against his chest and patting my back with his other big hand.

The chokes subsided, trailing off in a couple of helpless giggles. For the girl in the story, I had nothing but empathy; I probably felt right now the way she had then. But imagining that happening to Dimitri had me beside myself.

Maybe that made me a bad person, especially since he'd told me that story to make me feel better.

Meh. I could live with it.

"Sorry," I whispered, getting my voice to sort-of work at last. "I'm okay."

Dimitri's chest relaxed under me as he let out a long, slow exhale. "Okay. That's good. You believe me that it's no big deal? You really think I'd be more worried about how bad we are at getting ourselves mated than about you having a fucking seizure, Brook?"

Getting my sluggish thoughts in order proved as much of a

challenge as getting them to come off of my tongue, which felt like a sausage. A dry, overcooked sausage.

I should've pulled away and lain down on my own, or…really anything that didn't mean staying there in his arms, soaking up his heat and strength and support. But it felt so damn good. Maybe my father had been right all along, and I was a weak, pathetic loser.

Finally I managed, "Why would you care? I mean, you're, we're. We're not mated. Even if we were. It's not real."

A long silence fell, broken only by Dimitri's even breaths. Mine were still too quiet, still a little suppressed. The last time, that'd gotten better after a couple of hours, and I'd been totally fine after a good night's sleep, with only a lingering grogginess that a triple latte dispelled easily enough. I could only hope the same would hold true this time around.

"I don't know how many times I've got to tell you, you paid me to do a job," he replied at last, as if he'd been having the same trouble finding words and pushing them out of his mouth. "The job's to be your mate. Even if it's not real, like we fell all fucking in love or some shit like that, it's going to be real, like we have a mate bond. And we're working together for a goal. Your mate takes care of you. That's how it's supposed to be. A mate doesn't make fun of you or walk away when you're sick or you need somebody. I never planned to get mated, ever, but I swore if I did I wouldn't be a fucking asshole like—"

He cut off abruptly, leaving me stunned. He had told me more than once that he'd honor our agreement, but to me that'd meant cooperating by wearing what I told him to wear, going where I told him to go, and trying to impress my parents with what a classic alpha he was. Not…genuinely looking out for me.

And not to mention, he'd left me wildly curious, figuratively on the edge of my seat for the next couple of words—which didn't come.

"Like who?" I slurred, choosing to address that rather than wading into the minefield of his shocking, unexpected, and possibly undeserved turn for the caring and kind.

"Someone I used to know," he said, with quelling finality. "Doesn't matter. Point is, if I ever got mated, I was going to treat my mate well. You're going to be my mate, because that's my job. I'm going to treat you well, just because. Stop assuming I'm going to be a total prick because I'm an alpha and I look like a thug."

I managed to twist my head back against his shoulder, melting a little when he instantly accommodated me by tipping his arm at what had to be an uncomfortable angle so he could hold my head up without my neck getting hurt.

Still, I had to take issue with that last part of his statement. I raised my eyebrows pointedly, and he let out a wry chuckle.

"Yeah, okay. I look like one because I am one. You got me there. Still not the kind of prick who abuses his mate when he's not feeling well."

I studied him for a minute: the slight quirk to his lips, the steadiness and sincerity in those gorgeous gray eyes.

Abuse? Staying with me, holding me, comforting me, trying to reassure me, promising me that he'd take care of me…that fell pretty far from the abuse tree. He might've scared me when we met and antagonized me ever since, but looking at him now, and feeling so safe in his arms, it was hard to imagine him abusing anyone, ever. Especially someone he'd promised to take care of. That stubborn, determined set to his jaw suggested he might take what he saw to be his duty and responsibility to ridiculous lengths.

"What if I went crazy and tried to kill you?"

That slight smile widened into a grin. "*Tried* is the operative word there, Brook. Good luck with that. I guess I'd pin you down and sit on you until you stopped trying."

Right. Such an abusive prick.

How had I, who'd screwed up my personal life in every possible way, managed to go through a seedy fixer to set myself up with a criminal for a mate and still stumble on someone as decent, underneath all the offers to murder people, as Dimitri?

And honestly. Offering to murder Blake, shock value aside, didn't take much of the bloom off the rose for me. That seemed like such a sensible, normal reaction to Blake's existence. Most people who'd met him and many who hadn't had no doubt considered it.

I really had misjudged him. Completely. And now I had to move forward and try to do better on my end. No more needling him over bullshit. No more interpreting everything he said in the worst possible spirit. If he pissed me off, I'd remind myself of this moment, when he'd offered me more by way of comfort and sympathy and actual help than all of my nearest and dearest relatives combined had done, ever.

"Do thugs get their not-quite-mates a glass of water and help them stagger to the bathroom? Is that part of the Dimip—Pechor," I stopped, the stammer tripping up my tongue. He waited patiently. I swallowed hard and tried again. "Dimitri Pechorin service package?"

"Thugs-R-Us. We beat people up and we do in-home care on the side, because we're flexible like that and we really need the money," he said dryly, drawing a laugh out of me. "Come on. Let's get you sorted out and back in bed. You're going to sleep for a while, huh?"

"Yeah." I tried to struggle my way up, and Dimitri boosted me all the way to sitting, sliding out from behind me and balancing me as I swung my feet over the side of the bed. "Shit," I said as realization hit. "I'm still naked."

He rolled his eyes at me. "Uh-huh. I'll avert my eyes, princess. Let's get this show on the road."

"Don't call me that," I groused, but halfheartedly. I didn't have the energy for more. And the floor felt like some indescribably weird and unpleasant lumpy thing under my bizarrely oversensitive feet. Ugh. Fuck my brain.

"You going to make it to the bathroom on your own?"

Well, fine then. "Whatever," I muttered. "I guess you can call me whatever you want. Just don't call me Shirley."

Dimitri laughed and helped me up, and we staggered toward the bathroom.

At least he had good taste in movies. That and his determination to take care of me…well, I'd had worse friends and lovers. Much worse.

We'd make this work.

Chapter 6

It Gets Bigger

That can-do attitude lasted until the late morning of the next day.

I'd slept the rest of Friday plus all night, finally waking up at the unthinkably late hour of eight-thirty on Saturday morning. Usually I had an alarm for six-thirty and woke up half an hour before that. Even on weekends.

Dimitri emerged from the guest room across the hall as soon as I stirred, standing in the hallway between our open bedroom doors and running a hand through his messy hair to get it out of his face.

The bastard looked like an underwear advertisement.

I probably looked like someone had dragged me backward through a couple of hedges.

"Hungry?" he said. "I'm starving. I'm going to figure out if you have anything in your kitchen if you don't need any help."

I shook my head, the thought of Dimitri's "help" in the shower, or with getting dressed, making my blood run cold. Yeah, he might be shockingly sympathetic and nonchalant. But I'd humiliated myself quite enough, thank you.

He nodded and headed downstairs without bothering to put on pants. Thank God my mother would've left early this morning. She tended to show up on my doorstep, since I only lived a few houses away.

I managed a shower—and I washed as thoroughly as the day before, determined that nothing was going to stand in the way of getting the mating done and dusted today—and a set of clean clothes, a pair of nice jeans and a polo shirt since I didn't intend to go out anywhere that required a suit. Dimitri raised his eyebrows at me when I appeared in the kitchen, but he didn't comment.

So sue me. I didn't really do casual.

And then he put an omelet in front of me. I fell on it like the ravenous wolf I was, too hungry to even thank him or marvel at the fact that my fridge had contained eggs and cheese.

"You ready?" Dimitri asked as I pushed my plate away and drained the last of my coffee; he'd found the coffee maker, too, and brewed it even stronger than I usually did.

Yeah, maybe we really could make this work. I got up, ignoring the churning of nerves in my belly, and went back upstairs, with Dimitri following close enough behind me that I could feel the heat of him. Part of me wanted to skitter away, but the rest of me…apparently yesterday's debacle had been enough to condition me to the idea that Dimitri's body equaled safety.

Would it really be so bad to close my eyes, relax, and let him deal with fucking me? He'd offered.

"Have you ever had anal sex?" I forced the words out before I could think better of them, and it helped that I didn't have to look him in the eye while I said them.

A low chuckle raised the hairs on the back of my neck. "Probably at least as much as you have. Don't worry. I know what I'm doing."

"What?" I spun around and glared at him, hands on my hips. The way he stared me down, calm and sardonic, reminded me why I'd wanted to have this conversation facing away. Damn it. "You told me you're not gay! Not even a little bit bi!"

He sighed. "Women also like anal sex. News flash. And I've slept with a lot of them. How much action do you get, anyway? You never do anything but work."

"That's—that's—" Totally inaccurate. Not…completely accurate, anyway. Fuck it. "I get laid!"

This time I got a snort of laughter instead of a sigh, and he crossed his massive arms over his broad chest, raising one skeptical eyebrow.

"You're about to, anyway."

Anything else I could've said withered on my tongue.

He had me there. And I had to hope he wasn't lying about his experience, because I wouldn't be continuing that subject even if it meant my father would retire on the spot.

I spun on my heel and went into my room, pulling off my shirt and dropping it on top of the dresser before I turned around again.

And that was when my confidence in our ability to make it work evaporated into thin air and also ran away screaming.

Dimitri had already shucked his T-shirt and boxers. His cock clearly didn't feel more than the very mildest of interest, hanging almost entirely limp against his thigh. And he still looked like that really quick shot from the end of that dumb movie about the 70s porn stars, where they finally showed a gasping audience what all the fuss had been about for the last two and a half hours.

"There is no fucking way in hell we're going to make this work," I muttered, unable to tear my eyes away.

"It gets bigger, especially when I knot," Dimitri said unhelpfully. And then added, even more unhelpfully, "Sorry."

Yeah. "I'm going to let you handle this. Lie back and think of England. That's what you suggested, right?" I unfastened my jeans and shoved them and my own boxers down to the floor, stepping out of them and leaving them where they lay. "Consider this part of the job."

I glanced over my shoulder as I turned to get on the bed, and I caught the strangest expression on Dimitri's face. He wasn't checking me out—I knew what that looked like. But he was examining me, head cocked a little, frowning as he surveyed my whole body from head to toe.

"Sure," he said at last, as I settled down on the bed on my stomach, head turned so I didn't suffocate in my pillows. "Part of the job."

My skin prickled with awareness as he climbed onto the bed from the end, and my whole body felt flushed and heavy. When his knees brushed the insides of my legs as he moved up and into position, I flinched.

"I'm not going to hurt you," he said. The bed dipped as he shifted his weight. A warm, callused hand landed on the small of my back, pinning me in place. "Settle down."

The heat and weight of his hand filled my entire consciousness, and I wanted to writhe and scream, crawl out from under him and run the fuck away.

But he'd told me to settle down, and so I did, seething with nervous energy but held together and held down by the force of his voice more than the physical pressure itself.

The lube cap clicked. He'd opened it one-handed, so how could he put it on that same hand…that question was answered when a cold trickle hit the crack of my ass instead. I gasped, jolted, and bit my lip hard. Fuck. That felt so strange. Two points of consciousness now: the hand on my back, so hot, and the slick, sticky wetness sliding down toward my hole, all cold and making me shiver.

I had to brace myself, digging my fingers into the sheets and gritting my teeth, because I knew what was coming next.

And it did, a thick, strong finger pressing between my cheeks, swiping up some of the lube and then pushing against the tender skin of my hole. Dimitri slipped the tip of his finger inside, and I clamped down involuntarily, my body trying to keep him out and only succeeding in doubling the sensation of penetration.

"Easy," he rumbled. "This isn't about anything but mating, remember? We don't have to enjoy it. That means there's nothing to be nervous about, right?"

And weirdly, those words accomplished what none of my previous partner in this act's reassurances and efforts to give me pleasure had done: they relaxed me. My eyes popped open, giving me a soothing view of my white pillowcase and off-white wall. Just like being at a spa, right? Lying on the table. Massages might hurt sometimes, but they helped your overall well-being—not that I'd taken the time to go get one for a couple of years, but still. I'd used to like them, even when the pain of having those tense muscles worked over by strong hands made me bite my lips to hold in a groan.

Pleasure wasn't the point of this. I knew I'd hate it. So why fight it? Besides, Dimitri wouldn't be offended or have his feelings hurt the way a real boyfriend would if I lay there like a lump and simply took his cock in stoic silence.

It was incredibly freeing.

"Yeah," I said, my voice hitching as he pushed his finger deeper. "You're actually right about that."

A twist of his finger had me gasping again, but then he started working it in and out, steadily, like a piston in a well-timed engine.

"I'm right about a lot of things." He slid his finger out almost all the way and a second joined it, both of them demanding entry. "You'll see."

"Too much," I gritted out, as my ass stretched around those two big fingers.

"Nope, you can take it."

"What—that's not your call to ma—" I cut myself off with a moan as both fingers worked their way into me.

"See? Right about that too." His smugness deserved a sharp retort, but pressed down into the bed by the strength of one of his hands while the other finger-fucked me, I didn't have a lot of recourse. "You're stretching open just fine, Brook."

Something in the deep rasp of his voice as he said that made me shudder, my hips coming up off the bed as if I wanted to get him deeper, my body responding to him in a way that my mind couldn't begin to control—or comprehend.

But my nerves had settled, my anxiety unraveling and fluttering away into the ether. Dimitri had taken charge of the situation. An alpha had it all figured out.

Where the hell had that thought come from? The whole point of this exercise was to wrest my life and my career away from alphas who didn't know what they were doing, or at best had their heads so far up their own alpha asses that they couldn't see beyond their own knots.

But Dimitri had cared for me yesterday. He'd proven himself.

And whether or not I wanted to submit to him, put myself in his hands, my instincts were against me.

He poured more lube over his fingers, down into me, and this time the cool of it soothed the burn of my strained muscles and skin. Two fingers became three, pumping in and out of me easily now, the squelching sound of the motion loudly obscene in the quiet room.

Dimitri didn't bother asking if I was okay, or telling me what he was going to do next. I was a thing he was using to accomplish our mutual goal of mating and getting this over with, not an equal participant.

And my eyes drifted shut, the last of the tension draining out of me. My cock hadn't so much as stirred, and that was totally fine. It didn't need to. No one needed me to do anything at all. No demands. No requirements. No one hassling me or expecting me to make any decisions.

I could simply exist here, with Dimitri's hands on and in my body.

When he pulled his fingers out, he traced his fingertip around the stretched-out rim of my hole. So gentle, for a man like that.

His knees pushed me wider, nudging my thighs apart. "Lift your hips for me," he said softly. "Ass in the air, Brook."

Christ. I obeyed, knowing it'd be easier for both of us if I did, but exposing myself like that felt so fucking *wrong*. His thick cockhead pressed against my hole, the tip lodging there for a moment before he shifted his grip, took my hips in both hands, and thrust, hard and long and deep. It felt like he'd shifted everything inside my body to make room for him with that one smooth motion.

This wasn't just an object in me, the way it'd been the other two times I'd been fucked. This was a *cock*, a big one, hot and vital and a part of the alpha holding me still for him to take. It'd been so disconnected, last time. The thing in me, and the man putting it there, like they were separate. This time I knew it was Dimitri's cock in me, and I couldn't forget it was him fucking me.

My head buzzed with that knowledge, overwhelming and impossible to escape, exactly the way I couldn't escape the physicality of it.

Another buzzing sort of sensation started to build, a tension and awareness inside me where his cock pressed and rubbed over more inches of my flesh than I'd thought I had in there. It almost burned, except that the heat didn't hurt me. My cock twitched a little, my balls heavy with a sweet, deep ache.

My eyes opened again, staring in horror. For fuck's sake. No. No, I would not start to get aroused by Dimitri fucking me mechanically because I'd paid him a hundred thousand dollars to do it. He was probably picturing a hot woman, eyes closed and mind a million miles away. I mean, I'd never had a thing for women, but I could've stayed hard with one if she'd let me fuck her up the ass and I hadn't had to do a lot of touching. Dimitri didn't want me.

Every snap of his hips drove that huge cock deeper, filling me so completely I could hardly think about anything else. My body rubbed over the sheets, my face pushed into the pillow rhythmically, I was splayed open with his hips pressing into my thighs, Christ, and now that heat in me had grown to an inferno. I writhed under him, trying to stop it. Trying to get away from my body's betrayal.

I'd never wanted to be fucked. I'd never even thought about playing with my ass or trying to get off that way. Getting fucked hadn't done a damn thing for me when I'd tried it.

The slap of skin on skin echoed off the ceiling, my own panting, too-rough gasps a shameful counterpoint.

Dimitri didn't make a sound. His fingers dug into my hips, ten points of not-quite-pain.

Pressure built inside me, desperate to find some kind of release.

He went faster and faster, finally letting out a punched-out groan as he came, a flood of heat that forced a startled cry out of me.

And then I felt it: his knot, swelling inside my body, stretching my hole so much I moaned from the pain and the strangeness of it, and pushing—pushing on that spot—my muscles locked up, and I convulsed with a surge of pain-pleasure-release that I couldn't control, that swept me away with it irresistibly.

My still-soft cock spread wetness under my stomach, hot and shocking, as my head spun and that horrible, unwanted orgasm twisted me in in its grip, shooting pleasure down every nerve and whiting out my vision.

Through the haze—and the continuing heavy pressure of Dimitri's knot, which had only gotten *bigger*, oh my God, had he ever not been exaggerating about that—I felt him let go of my hips and lean down, setting his mouth over the curve of my neck and shoulder. His hot breath seared my neck. The scrape of his fangs had me tensing, squeezing my eyes shut…and then he bit down, sharp and burning, more than a physical sensation. Tendrils of magic unfurled from his fangs, swirling through my blood and his, binding us together. Consciousness of everything about Dimitri soaked into me, from the heat and weight of his physical body to a hint of the workings of his mind, vigorous and focused.

The bond made us one entity, magically speaking, fused and connected at too many points to count. His knot throbbed, the bite throbbed, and I moaned, ending in a drawn-out whimper, stretched to my breaking point by too many kinds of oversensitivity at once.

Dimitri's arm wrapped around my chest and he tugged me against him, slumping down on top of me, his teeth sliding out of my torn flesh.

And then we lay there, both of us panting for breath, the sweat cooling on our skin, wrapped so closely in one another that neither our bodies nor our souls could have been separated.

Mated.

Chapter 7

I'll Be Expecting More

At last, the overwhelming sensory input from the formation of the mating bond faded slightly, and I opened my eyes and tried to readjust to reality. Same white pillow. Same off-white wall. The familiar sounds from outside: a lawnmower in the distance, the buzz of a helicopter passing overhead. Birds chirping in the tree by my bedroom window.

But it all hit me at a slight angle, off-kilter. Like the world had shifted around me, only I knew it hadn't. I was the one who'd changed.

And I had Dimitri wrapped around me, his cock buried inside me, and his bite on my neck.

A shudder ran through me, and Dimitri stiffened. "Fuck, please tell me you're not having another seizure," he said roughly, his breath ruffling my hair. "You were shaking when we fucked, too, and your muscles clenched up. Dammit, if I'd known I wouldn't—"

"I'm fine," I whispered. For a certain value of fine, anyway. "Not a seizure."

Every cell in my body tingled and twitched. But not because of Hensley's.

"Okay. Let's roll over so I can lie down without crushing you."

"No, wait—"

But it was too late, and he'd already moved his arm, slipping his hand down toward my stomach to hold me in place, probably so his knot wouldn't damage me by tugging out when we moved.

He went still again, his hand resting against my betrayingly sticky skin. "So. Not a seizure starting when we were fucking."

"I said it wasn't, didn't I?"

"No need to get defensive."

"I'm not defensive!"

Dimitri laughed, shaking my whole body and particularly jostling my tender insides.

"Ow!" I shoved my ass back against him, trying desperately to keep his knot in place.

"Sorry." He tightened his grip around my waist and finally rolled us over onto our sides, slipping his other arm under my head. It did not feel good. At all. Warm and solid and supporting me in the perfect position to relax. But not good. I tried to hold myself up a little, but then Dimitri petted my belly, and I gave in and let my head flop against his bicep. "See? This isn't so bad. It even made you come. Win-win."

"It didn't make me come," I gritted out, even though he could feel the evidence for himself. "That was some kind of weird...reflex. A mating thing."

"A mating thing."

The heavy skepticism in his tone had me itching to smack him in the face. Simultaneously, I wanted nothing so much as to snuggle down and sleep for a week wrapped securely in his arms.

That was definitely a mating thing.

"Yeah, a mating thing. You seemed to enjoy it, right? So it's not just me."

Dimitri's arm tightened around my waist. "You have an incredibly tight ass. Made it a little easier to stay hard."

I let out a sigh, very slowly, forcing my blood pressure to stay at a normal level. What had I been expecting, hearts and flowers? I'd known my prospective mate wasn't exactly the poetic type, and I didn't like that kind of thing anyway.

We had a job to do. We'd accomplished the first step. And I needed to be satisfied with that—and yeah, it made me smile to think of how nonplussed my father would be when he found out I'd chosen my own damn alpha, thank you—forget everything else, and move on to the next part of my plan.

"Glad it wasn't too awful for you," I said, keeping the sarcasm in my tone dialed down to an impressive four or so on a scale of ten. "As soon as we're not tied together, we need to talk about what happens when we tell my parents. Make some plans."

"You're the boss," he said without any bite. "Big, dumb, polite, and silent. I'm just following orders here."

Well, that showed the proper spirit, at least.

And if his sarcasm had edged closer to a six out of ten, I could pretend to ignore it.

I closed my eyes and let myself drift for a bit, relaxing into the cradle of Dimitri's big body. Fuck it. I could take a nap before we got anything else done.

***

After we'd pried our bodies apart, showered, and dressed—and napped for half an hour, an unimaginable luxury that made me nearly panicky with the feeling of having neglected my responsibilities—I dropped Dimitri off at the cheap motel he'd been staying in. He promised to come back to my place within an hour with his car and his belongings, and he was right on time, carrying nothing but a big duffel bag and a coat over his arm.

I'd basically doubled everything he owned by taking him shopping, which gave me a strange, protective feeling I didn't want to examine too closely.

So all of a sudden, there he was. In my house. The scent of him had already started to permeate the whole place, alpha pheromones and a hint of rich, tart citrus teasing my nose every time I turned around. Dimitri went out again and came home with groceries. Real groceries, not the box of cardboardy cereal and old mustard that'd comprised my entire stock of food after he'd used everything edible for those omelets.

Because I'd taken Friday off, I really did have work to do, and I hid myself away in my office for a couple of hours, grimly wading through emails until I couldn't stand to sit anymore. Any actual soreness had healed already; that was one of those advantages of a werewolf physiology that I forgot to think about most of the time. I had no idea how humans dealt with getting fucked up the ass.

But every time I shifted in my chair, it reminded me of what we'd done. It didn't hurt, but it was as if now that I'd been knotted—and come helplessly on that knot, a thought I wanted to avoid—I couldn't stop thinking about a part of my body that I'd been mostly blissfully oblivious to all my life.

Finally, the tantalizing scents of meat and onions and some other things I couldn't pin down, combined with my discomfort, got me up and heading for the stairs.

I found Dimitri in the kitchen drinking a beer, the bottle raised to his lips with his left hand while his right neatly flipped something white and floppy out of a pan and onto a waiting plate. He swallowed, put the bottle down, and grinned at me over his shoulder.

"Good timing. I thought I'd have to come and drag you away from that bullshit."

"It's not bullshit," I protested reflexively, even though honestly, most of it was. "What's that? Are those crepes?"

He said something quickly in Russian that didn't sound like a real word. I manfully resisted saying *bless you*. At my look of total confusion, he repeated more slowly, "Blinchiki." He shrugged. "Crepes, if you want to be all stupid and French about it."

Crepes? Dimitri Pechorin knew how to make *crepes*?

I made a face at him, but I couldn't resist the incredible smells, and I crossed to the stove, trying to stay out of his personal space as much as possible. Just because we were mated now, it didn't mean we needed to get all touchy-feely. The normal amount of distance I'd give a roommate. That was the way to go.

Even if he smelled nearly as good as dinner.

Stupid mating bond.

The stove held two frying pans, one for the crepe-things and one for potatoes, pork, and onions, all sizzling together in a way that promised the best kind of caloric deliciousness. God, I loved some things about Russian culture. They'd never seen a vegetable they didn't want to ignore in favor of meat.

In fact, I wasn't entirely sure they'd ever seen a green vegetable at all other than cabbage.

Either way, I approved wholeheartedly.

"So you kill people, you do in-home care for Hensley's patients, and you cook," I said. "What other talents are you hiding?"

A sticky sort of silence descended on the kitchen, emphasized by the hiss and spit of the pan and the tick of the clock on the wall.

"How many people do you think I've killed, exactly?" he asked at last, his tone painfully flat and neutral.

Well, fuck. I glanced up at him through my eyelashes. That cheerful grin had vanished, replaced by a downturned mouth and set jaw.

I'd meant it as a joke. Apparently he hadn't taken it that way.

"You did offer to kill Blake the day we met," I offered tentatively. "It didn't seem like so much of a stretch?"

Another silence.

"One," Dimitri said at last. "It was self-defense, mostly. Worst way to put it was that it was a fair fight. You probably don't believe me, since I guess every murdering asshole would say the same thing. But I've never killed anyone for money."

The right reaction to that probably would've been horror, or disgust, or at best dismay.

All I felt was a surge of vicious partisanship. Of course it'd been self-defense. Of course it'd been a fair fight.

Jesus, this mating bond had me all twisted into knots.

But looking up at him, remembering how gently he'd handled me last night and today...I didn't have it in me to condemn him, even if he *was* bending the truth to make himself look better.

And given how blunt he'd been with me so far, I doubted it anyway.

"I believe you. But why would you suggest that? I mean, why—if that's not you. Why would you bring it up? Blake, I mean."

Dimitri picked up a wooden spoon from the counter and prodded at the potatoes in the pan. Stalling? "I have a shitty sense of humor, I guess. And I wanted to see how you'd react. I figured I'd give you what you thought you were getting," he added abruptly. "You know. Live down to the obvious expectations."

That hit me like a frying pan to the face.

Live down to the obvious expectations. Didn't that just strike a chord, so deep in me that the vibrations took a second to get to the surface. I'd spent my whole life struggling with being more than the judgments of those around me, and never having anyone recognize it. Not an alpha. Not the perfect son. Never good enough, no matter what I did.

"Well, you've set a standard you'll have to live up to, now," I said, my voice rough with emotion I couldn't hide. "You took care of me. And apparently you cook. So I'll be expecting more from now on. You'll just have to deal with that."

I felt—a lightening, like a weight had lifted somewhere I couldn't quite define. It took a moment for me to realize that wasn't me: it was Dimitri, his own emotion transferring through the mate bond.

I'd done that. For him.

And my satisfaction, my pleasure in that, leached into the mate bond from my end, brightening it in the edges of my senses.

Dimitri shifted a little closer to me, the heat of his body soothing my physical senses, too.

I tipped my head up, unable to help a smile from spreading across my face. Being mated wasn't so terrible, was it? Like having a roommate who cooked, and maybe even a friend. An ally.

He gazed down at me, his eyes glowing faintly, expression unreadable. His lips parted, and he leaned down a fraction of an inch.

And then the doorbell screeched, a horrible up-and-down pseudo-musical tone that made us jump apart, breathing hard and staring at each other in shock, whatever weird spell the bond had cast over us abruptly shattered.

"The fuck," Dimitri growled. "Who the fuck? You expecting a package?"

I already got yours. I choked on a horrible burst of hysterical laughter, because a cheesy porno this was not, and if I couldn't keep my tongue under control this was about to be a hundred times more awkward than it already couldn't help being.

Because I knew who was at the door.

And if my mother had cut her spa weekend short to come and check on me, we were in so much fucking trouble. This kind of casual domesticity with a man they hadn't met and wouldn't want me to mate in the first place would horrify her. She'd see it as vulgar and low-class, not to mention the shock of her plans being disrupted.

I had to control the narrative. Introducing Dimitri like this when I hadn't planned it out to the nth degree could be disastrous.

"Go upstairs and get some clothes on," I hissed. "Quickly! Something decent! Jeans are okay, but like…like what I'm wearing. I know I bought you a polo shirt."

"What—who is it? And I'm not wearing that! The fuck do you think we are, the Bobbsey Twins?"

"You're in your underwear!" It came out almost a moan. "That's my—oh, fuck." I'd caught my father's voice, a faint, discontented rumble. "Shit! It's both of them!"

"Both of—" And then it twigged, and his mouth fell open and stayed that way. "Shit. Okay. Clothes."

He dashed out of the kitchen, with me chivvying him along and whispering demands that he hurry.

But it didn't matter. We were both still in the living room when a key clicked in the lock, the door opened, and my parents stepped through from the foyer, identical expressions of irritation on their faces that quickly morphed into shock as they took in the scene in front of them.

That was when I realized Dimitri was still holding the spoon.

Well, this was going to go poorly. So much for the best-laid plans of mice, men, and werewolves.

Chapter 8

A United Front

"Explain yourself," my father said heavily. "I understood that you were too unwell to deign to go to the office yesterday. And now we find you capering around the house with…someone like this."

Ah. So it wasn't only Dimitri coming in and out of the gate that'd triggered this parental "concern." My day off had rung some alarm bells, apparently.

I opened my mouth, even though my mind was spinning like a hamster in a creaky wheel and I had no fucking clue what to say, but Dimitri got there before me. "It's traditional to spend some time alone with your new mate, and I decided to humor Brook when he wanted the day off." *Humor* me? The *fuck*? "Maybe you should explain why you came in without waiting for us to open the door. You're lucky a little capering is all you walked in on."

My head went light and floaty, spots swimming in my vision. We should've been at my parents' place by appointment, dressed perfectly, a cool and collected power couple making our announcement like adults.

Instead, here we were. Capering. In our underwear—one of us, anyway. With a wooden spoon.

My mother's mouth dropped open, and one perfectly-manicured hand flew up to cover it. Her light blue eyes, so much like Blake's, went wide.

And my father…his square-jawed face flushed nearly purple as he stared Dimitri down, one hand flexing as if he needed to restrain his claws. He didn't have the height most alphas did, being only an inch or two taller than me. But he had the broad shoulders, heavy muscles, and attitude of the typical alpha, and the way his body had stiffened inside his ever-present gray suit spelled trouble.

"You should introduce us, Brook," Dimitri went on before I

could intervene. What had happened to my voice? It was like my vocal cords had been paralyzed. "Since we're family now, and everything."

"Family?" my mom choked out, just as my father finally exploded with, "You have no call to tell my son what to—"

He cut off with an incoherent sound as Dimitri moved, taking one prowling step forward, putting himself between me and my parents, the spoon somehow becoming threatening with the way he had it gripped in his hand.

"I'm his alpha," Dimitri growled, raising the hairs on the back of my neck. "He may be your son, but he's my mate. I have call to tell him anything I want. And right now, I'm telling him to introduce us. Or you can leave."

Christ, what was the matter with him? How dare he speak for me like that! But the other half of me, the cowardly half that couldn't speak up for myself anyway, absolutely fucking loved it. My alpha, defending...no, not defending me. Taking over. Taking control, exactly the way I didn't want him to!

But I couldn't put myself between two angry alphas. My spine tried to crawl out of my back and slither away at the thought of it, and I could only stand there, still frozen, fists clenched at my sides to keep my own claws from sprouting, and wait, either for them to fight or for one of them to back down.

The stare-down seemed to last forever. My father's eyes weren't glowing, because they rarely did—he said a real alpha didn't need to posture like that. But everything else in his body language bristled with rage.

And then he backed down.

He stepped back, standing next to my mother, yielding to Dimitri.

I couldn't believe it.

"You should introduce your alpha, Brook," my father said, very low. "Since he's now a part of my pack."

His slight emphasis on *my* pack made it clear that he wanted us to think he was making a gracious concession, as the real alpha in the room.

I wasn't fooled.

And I doubted Dimitri was either.

But he smoothly transferred the spoon to his left hand, managing not to make it look silly—and absently, I realized that this was what my father always overcompensated for, his inability to show this kind of effortless command of a situation—and turned to me, raising an eyebrow.

Right. My cue.

To do what the alphas were telling me to do.

And if I refused, or showed any unhappiness about it, I'd look like a brat with no self-control.

I felt cold, and small, and insignificant, and I'd done this to myself. Engineered this situation on purpose, thinking that somehow it'd be better than if I let my father engineer it for me.

"This is Dimitri Pechorin, my mate," I said, forcing the words out of my dry throat. "Dimitri, my father, Boyd Castelli, leader of the Castelli Pack and CEO of Castelli Industries. My mother, Whitney Castelli."

"Pleased to meet you," Dimitri murmured, shaking first my father's hand and then, after her palpable hesitation, my mother's. And then he nearly gave me a heart attack. "We were about to have dinner. Want to stay? There's more than enough. I made blinchiki, you know, Russian crepes."

"*You* cooked," my father said disbelievingly, with a curl of his lip.

Right. Because real alphas didn't know how to use a stove.

My mother glanced at him, biting her lip. "Russian caviar is appropriate with crepes," she put in. Trying to defuse the situation? Being passive-aggressive? God, they were so dysfunctional. I couldn't even tell anymore when they were sniping at each other or not. Or when they were sniping at me.

"No caviar," Dimitri said. "Brook doesn't like it."

And then he turned his head and shot me the faintest twitch of a smile.

He'd remembered. That offhand remark I'd made when he was needling me about the silver spoon in my mouth. He'd remembered, and he'd made it clear that he knew more about what I liked than my own parents did.

I took the couple of steps to close the distance between us, wrapping my hand around his bicep and—not quite cuddling up to him. But almost. Maybe we could present a united front after all.

"You're more than welcome to stay for dinner," I said. "If you don't have time tonight, we can come to dinner with you in a day or two. I'd like you to get to know Dimitri properly."

My father looked from me to Dimitri and then back again, fixing me with a cold, acrimonious glare that almost had me cringing and dropping my eyes.

Almost.

Because this time, I had Dimitri's solid, bolstering presence at my side, his hard muscles under my hand. My fingers tensed, digging in hard enough to hurt someone other than an alpha were. Dimitri leaned almost imperceptibly closer to me.

And that gave me the courage to look my father in the eye and lift my chin, facing him down in a way I never had before.

"The time to get to know him properly would have been before this absurd mating, Brook," my father snarled. "We will be discussing this at length. You will come to see me tomorrow, in the office, at seven sharp. Do you understand?"

"I'll be there," I said, my stomach churning. The office, at seven in the morning, on a Sunday. It was a clear power play.

And it had worked, because he had all the power when it came to anything involving the company or my attendance there.

Dimitri shifted at my side, clearly about to speak up, and I squeezed his arm even harder. *Shut up.* He got it, thankfully, but I could feel his irritation through the bond and through the tension that stiffened him at my side.

My mother kept her mouth shut, too. Her husband had made his decree; she'd follow it. That was how the Castellis did things.

After a moment of even more painful, tense awkwardness, my father said, "We're leaving, Whitney." And he turned to the door and opened it without saying goodbye or acknowledging us again in any way.

The door slammed behind them.

I realized I was standing there, eyes closed, breathing deeply and clinging to Dimitri's arm like I never intended to let him go.

I let him go in a big hurry, dropping his arm as if it'd burned me and stumbling back a step or two, needing to get the hell away from him before whatever his proximity had done to damage my brain became permanent.

"What the hell was that?" I demanded, stumbling mentally and emotionally as much as physically but determined to regain a little bit of my footing, in every respect. "You acted like you were—you—my *alpha*? *I have call to tell him anything I want*? What the fuck, Dimitri?"

He turned, face expressionless. "I thought that was what you hired me for."

"I told you I was in charge! Except for the mating itself, I was the one in control. You're here to back me up, to make me look good! Not to do exactly what my father wanted an alpha of his choosing to do with me!"

I stopped, panting for breath, chest heaving. Horrifyingly, I seemed to be on the verge of tears, so much rage and frustration welling up in me that I almost choked on it.

Dimitri stepped forward, knuckles white around the spoon, and I stumbled again, unable to stand my ground.

He stopped dead, face gone white, eyes glowing gold. "For fuck's sake, Brook, I'm not going to hurt you! I would never hurt you."

"Okay, so you wouldn't hurt me, but you don't have any problem with treating me like a kid, or a subordinate, or—a possession. You're exactly the same as he is!" That feeling still lingered, the sensation of safety and security and courage I'd had when I pressed myself up to his side and held on to him. And it only made this so much worse. Now that it'd faded a little, I saw how he'd betrayed me—how I'd betrayed myself by going along with it. "You're exactly the same," I repeated, the last word trailing off in a hitch of my breath that I couldn't control.

Enough. Fuck. I'd done this to myself. And I pushed past him, nearly blinded by tears, needing to get upstairs and lock myself in my bedroom, or my office, or anywhere I could be alone.

Strong hands caught my upper arms, and there was a thump as the spoon finally hit the floor. I struggled, thrashing and shouting, but Dimitri wrapped his arms tightly around my body, pinned my arms, and crushed me against him, hard and hot and too big to fight.

And I had to give in, going limp in his hold, tears streaming down my cheeks at last. I'd wanted to get away before he saw them.

Now he'd know how weak I truly was, how much I deserved the way he'd treated me.

He started to move, and I didn't resist. We ended up on the couch a few feet away, Dimitri dropping down and pulling me with him, almost into his lap.

I hated it. Hated the way my body wanted to relax into it and let him take over. Stop fighting, stop arguing.

I was so fucking tired.

Dimitri nuzzled my ear, rubbing his head against the side of mine like a big cat instead of the wolf I knew he was. Soothing me.

Condescending prick. He didn't want to touch me for his own sake.

But it still felt so good I could've stayed like that for hours.

"You've spent your whole life with your asshole of a father," he said at last, very quietly. Very evenly. "But you don't seem to know him all that well. Someone like that isn't going to change. He won't ever respect you the way you want him to. You get that, right? He didn't want you to have an alpha mate because it'd make you more important in his eyes. He wanted you to have an alpha mate because then someone else could take responsibility for controlling you, keeping you in line."

He was right, of course. Absolutely, inarguably right.

But that didn't give him a right.

"So you decided to just give him what he wanted." I had to stop and swallow down the bitter, searing taste of bile in my mouth. "You might as well control me? Since he's not going to respect me anyway."

Another nuzzle, and this time his lips lingered, brushing over the shell of my ear. I shivered, oddly, as the heat of it arrowed down into my belly and pooled there. What the hell was he doing?

"He's not going to respect you, even though you deserve it." Dimitri shifted his head, breathing hot against my earlobe, his arms tightening around me. "But I do, okay? And he might back off if I don't back down." Another brush of his lips, another shiver, and my abdomen felt molten. "And then you can do whatever you want, make any decisions you want with me running interference. That's why you paid me to do this. So I could put up an alpha front for you, and you call the shots from behind the scenes, yeah?"

Was that why I'd paid him to do this? Had I paid him to…hold me in his arms and cuddle me? No, I'd paid him to…my eyes drifted shut. I'd started having trouble remembering what exactly I'd paid him to do. What he'd said sounded reasonable.

I'd have to think about it later. When I had a clearer head.

"Fine," I managed. "You can let go of me now." I really didn't want him to. Of course I wanted him to, I didn't want to be held like this. Christ. "Seriously."

A second later, he let me go, unwrapping his arms from around me and getting up off the couch in one smooth motion. I had to brace myself on the cushions to keep from toppling right over, and blink a couple of times to bring everything back into focus.

Dimitri picked up the spoon, frowned at it, and then looked back down at me. "I'm going to reheat dinner. You going to eat with me? Since no one else wants to, apparently?"

He pulled an exaggerated grimace, and I couldn't help laughing. "I'll eat with you." My stomach rumbled, right on cue, and he grinned at me. "Apparently I'm hungry."

"I hope so, because I made my grandmother's recipe, and she'll roll over in her grave if you don't eat until you can't make it up the stairs."

He turned toward the kitchen, but I couldn't quite let it go. "Dimitri?" He turned back, eyebrows raised. "That was seriously all for show? You're not going to—I need to be able to be comfortable when we're alone. I hate being steamrolled. I've spent my whole life being steamrolled."

Dimitri sobered, his expression as serious as I'd ever seen it. "Brook, I swear to you, on my grandmother's grave and her recipe for blinchiki. I have no interest in telling you what to do. You're a grown man, not a dependent. Hired for a job, doing the job. Remember? I have enough trouble running my own life. Honestly, you calling the shots on this is kind of a vacation for me. You hired an alpha asshole to act like one on cue, and that's what I'm doing. Okay?"

When I smiled, I felt it down to my toes, the tension ebbing away. "Okay."

He nodded. "Then come and eat. You know, if you want. Far be it from me to give you any orders."

I followed him into the kitchen, still smiling. Maybe if I ate enough Russian food, I'd recover the mental energy I needed to plan that meeting with my father in the morning.

Because my poor display this evening notwithstanding, I had a plan. And I had no intention of letting him roll right over me this time around.

Chapter 9

The Best Defense

The glass and concrete front of Castelli Industries' main campus shone blindingly bright in the morning sun, which had risen about the same time I did. By the time I pulled into my assigned parking spot right in front, it'd gotten high enough to light the building up like a beacon.

Only a couple of other cars scattered the lot: my father's, of course, in its very special parking spot even closer to the entrance than the handicapped spaces—possibly illegal, but no one said anything—and also a couple of others farther back, belonging to security guards and janitors.

Dimitri had seen me off, much to my surprise. His absurdly rumpled bedhead, ferocious scowl, and slitted eyes had confirmed my impression of him as not much of a morning person. But he'd started the coffee machine while I took a shower, grunted something that sounded encouraging as he handed me a cup, and hadn't killed me.

Overall, not the worst way to be sent off at the crack of dawn to a meeting that promised to make me want to kill myself if no one else got there first.

Not that I thought my father would necessarily win this round. I gave it sixty-forty in my favor, because for once, I held enough cards to play the game. But I still had a trickle of nervous sweat on my spine. And I knew it'd get ugly.

I found my father in his office on the top floor, seated behind the broad, polished desk that never held more than a laptop and his cup of coffee.

He glanced up as I walked in, the sun pouring through the window highlighting the few threads of silver in his dark hair. Blake and I had both inherited our coloring from our blonde mother, although

I'd inherited, or perhaps copied, my father's dress sense: we'd managed to wear practically identical charcoal gray suits this morning. A deep frown scored lines between his brows and bracketed the corners of his mouth.

"Your judgment is clearly even less reliable than I'd thought," he said after I'd stood there uncomfortably for a long moment. "Mating without my consent or even my knowledge? And mating someone without any pedigree, any advantage to the family? You'll break this bond at once. Prescott is already preparing for the ritual."

That didn't surprise me in the least, even though he clearly meant it to blindside me. The night before, my father had taken me by surprise and at a disadvantage.

He'd obviously planned to have the same high ground this morning.

But I'd also planned for this eventuality, long before I ever set that first fateful meeting with Dimitri. And I might be a coward and something of a pushover when it came to my family, but I'd successfully completed a hundred business negotiations with clients at least as aggressive as my father.

Sometimes, the best defense was a good offense. And if I took a deep breath, I could feel my bond to Dimitri in the back of my soul, linking me to his uncompromising strength. If I focused on that, I could do this.

"Certainly, if you want to cause an immense scandal and make me completely unmateable in the future," I said as calmly as I could, even though my heart tripped in an unsteady rhythm, my breathing following along. "Everyone's going to think I'm damaged goods. There could be rumors. About my health, for example." My father flinched slightly at the word *health*, and I had to force myself not to show any triumph. A hit, a palpable hit! "Not to mention, you know how Jerry and Melissa feel about bonding for life."

Our two oldest and most hidebound board members had very strong feelings about upholding werewolf traditions. Without some unforgiveable transgression—and their list of what qualified for that would be limited to things like murdering someone else in the pack—bond-breaking rituals were anathema to them. And a lot of our clients were on the same page. My father had spent most of his life building up a network of stuffy, stick-in-the-mud shifters with whom he primarily did business.

And now it could bite him in the ass, with my blessing.

His face had grown darker and darker, a vein pulsing in his temple. He stood, leaning his fists on the desk, obviously wanting to intimidate me with his size.

For the first time, it didn't work so well. Yeah, he could physically dominate me if he wanted to.

But Dimitri had made him blink first last night. My father wasn't invincible.

"You're nothing without me, without this family, without this company," my father said, his voice thick with rage. "If you and your trailer trash alpha want to live happily ever after, be my guest. You can leave your employee badge with security on your way out."

That was a bluff, and I knew it, and he had to know I knew it. My confidence soared.

"I'm sure Anderson Electric will be thrilled to have their account manager replaced in the middle of their biggest project with us. Maybe Blake could take over? No, wait. He's in Key West maxing out every credit card he can get his hands on."

That vein went nuclear, bulging enough to be visible from space. A sudden spike of real worry pierced my bubble of giddy joy at finally, *finally* saying some of the things I'd had trembling on the tip of my tongue for years. Was I going to give him that stroke his doctor had been warning us about?

Anyway, I'd pushed him as far as possible, and then some. I had to compromise now. Dial it back, give him an out. Make it possible for him to save some face while he gave me what I wanted and what we both knew had to be inevitable.

"Of course I wouldn't be working with Anderson if you hadn't taught me everything I know," I said, in a more conciliatory tone. Humble, even though it made me sick to my stomach. "But they want a Castelli on their account. Of course they do. You've made our name synonymous with high-quality solutions. That's why they came to us in the first place."

They'd come to us in the first place because I'd aggressively courted their business and gotten us the account.

But details.

A little of the color had faded out of my father's violently flushed face, and he hadn't exploded yet. Okay, I was on the right track.

"Dimitri may not be the kind of man you'd pictured for me, but he's a real alpha." I bit my lip, choosing my words carefully. What I said next would either sell it, or completely ruin my chances of getting out of this conversation with what I wanted. "You saw how he stood up to you last night, even though he was obviously intimidated by you. Most other alphas, you roll right over them. Isn't that the kind of alpha you want guiding me as I take the next steps in my career? As I spend more time representing the Castelli pack in public?"

It nearly made me vomit describing Dimitri's role in my life as "guiding me," but I could see my words having the desired effect. My father went from furious to thoughtful while I spoke, still angry but starting to calm.

I had to go for the killing stroke. My father couldn't supervise me all the time, even though he desperately wanted to. He needed a younger Castelli here, carrying on the family legacy; he also needed an alpha presence to satisfy his narrow-minded idea of what the family legacy ought to be. And we both knew Blake would never step up.

"I think Dimitri would be willing to spend time with me here at the company, bolstering me in negotiations and keeping an eye on my decision-making," I went on, my belly clenching tighter and tighter. If it was possible to humiliate myself more deeply, I didn't want to know about it. But this was why I'd formed this plan. And I was *winning*, I could feel it. "He's my alpha. Having him by my side day to day would only make me and the company stronger."

I stopped while I was hopefully ahead, letting that sink in for a minute.

Without mentioning Hensley's or any of the complications that would arise from that eventually, I knew it had to be at the forefront of his mind. Other than me, he didn't have an option to take over from him when that became necessary.

And if I could let him make it look to the board, and to our clients, and to himself, like it had been at least kind of his own idea…

"Your mother and I will host the two of you tomorrow, at our home, along with the Sandovals," he said at last, and my breath caught as I stopped myself from letting out the gusty exhale my lungs wanted to release. The Sandovals were Jerry, his wife, their daughter, and her mate, a stuffed-shirt lawyer who played golf with Blake sometimes. All of them were a tough crowd to please. "If he manages to behave himself decently, I'll consider allowing you to remain mated to him. But I don't have a lot of faith in his ability to do that."

I had total faith in Dimitri's ability to behave decently, but his ability to behave to their picky, snobbish standard? Not so much. My chest clenched.

"We'll be there, and I assure you I wouldn't have mated him if he couldn't impress our board members and clients." Lie.

Maybe he knew that by the narrowing of his eyes, but he didn't call me on it. Well, he certainly knew how to give you enough rope to hang yourself with.

"Then there's no more to be said at present. I'm sure you have a great deal of work to finish after your little stunt on Friday. I've already alerted your assistant to be here by eight."

Christ, she didn't get paid enough for that. And neither did I, come to think of it. But I managed to nod, smile, and escape his office without gritting my teeth audibly.

I'd intended to go and work from home.

Looked like I'd be doing my penance—or the first part of it, anyway—by spending Sunday here.

***

Dimitri and I spent Sunday night—or what was left of it after I finally dragged myself home at eight following a full twelve hours without a break of working through client files—prepping him for the dinner party. He was more cooperative than I expected.

Well, sort of.

I'd already told him about my confrontation with my father, and he'd laughed his ass off. "I didn't know you were such a manipulative little weasel," he said, sounding like he didn't mean that as a compliment, exactly. I tried not to be hurt, and it helped when he added,

"You did good, Brook. But I so wasn't intimidated."

Yes, because to an alpha, that would be the main point to keep in mind. I didn't roll my eyes, but it was close.

"I know," I said, getting my own back by patting his arm condescendingly.

He glowered at me, but he paid attention and didn't complain when I set the table with a whole bunch of cutlery and wine glasses and gave him a briefing on what you drank with different types of food.

It was when we got to the dinner conversation portion of the tutorial that he started bitching.

"I'm not going to pretend to be something I'm not, and I'm not going to spend the whole night lying," he groused as I told him, admittedly for the third or fourth time, not to mention anything from his life before meeting me. Like, *anything*. "If they ask me where I go skiing or something, what am I supposed to say? I'm not a rich guy. I don't have a rich-guy past."

"Then you fudge, okay? You don't have to lie, exactly. You just don't have to tell the truth. You say something like: 'I've heard Aspen is great. Are you a skier?' And then you let them talk about themselves. People love talking about themselves." I rubbed at my temples, wishing I could take my glasses off and close my eyes. Werewolves weren't prone to headaches, but my eyesight gave me those, too. Lucky me. "If Jerry likes you, this whole plan falls into place. And he's not actually so bad. He's really old-school, but he kind of likes me. It helps that he thinks Blake is one step above something that lives under a rock."

Dimitri grunted, rolled his eyes, and nodded.

"All right, so Jerry's daughter is—"

"I think that's enough for tonight," he cut in. We were sitting on the couch, and I'd started to slump a little lower into the cushions. I forced myself bolt upright again. "Seriously, Brook, you're about to pass out."

I blinked at him, trying to clear my rapidly blurring vision.

"I'm fine."

He sighed, and before I could stop him, he reached up and snatched my glasses off my face, folding them neatly and putting them on the coffee table—out of my reach, when I tried to grab them back.

"You're not fine. Lie down, put your head on the end of the couch, close your eyes, and tell me about Jerry's stupid family that way."

How had he known my eyes were hurting me? Could he feel it through the bond? Or was he simply way more observant than I'd given him credit for? I did what he told me, and I felt a lot better, the throbbing in the front of my skull easing and my body starting to relax.

By the time I'd finally emptied my head of everything I knew about Jerry's stupid family, I'd drifted halfway to dreamland, and I didn't resist when Dimitri took my hand, pulled me up and off the couch, and chivvied me up the stairs.

If Jerry liked him half as much as I did, I thought sleepily as I fell into bed, we were home free.

My eyes popped open, and I stared wide-eyed into the darkness.

Liking Dimitri wasn't supposed to be part of the plan. I was using him for a purpose, just like he was using me for money. Getting along okay, sure. That was great and necessary. But…more than that? It gave me a miserable, unsettled feeling in the pit of my stomach.

And it took me a while to calm down and go to sleep after all.

Chapter 10

If Not, No Worries

The door shut behind us, and Dimitri and I practically ran for it, speed-walking down the brick pathway leading from my parents' porch to the sidewalk. We'd managed to get out before Jerry and his wife, thus dodging any kind of tense conversation alone with my parents; Jerry had opportunely told my father they needed a word alone about some board politics. I could have kissed him.

"Oh, my God," I gasped, as we rounded the corner of the hedge and escaped. My heart pounded away, giddy relief throwing it, and me, into a tizzy. "We got out alive. I can't fucking believe it."

Dimitri grinned down at me, finally looking like himself as he did. He'd put on such a good show. Un-fucking-believably good. He'd slicked his hair back and worn one of the suits I'd picked out for him, a dark blue that brought out the little flecks of green in his gray eyes. Jerry, unbeknownst to me, had studied Russian literature as an undergrad, something he mentioned after I'd introduced my mate. Dimitri had pulled some weird details about the town Dostoevsky had used for the setting of *The Brothers Karamazov* out of his ass, going on for a couple of minutes about the history of Russian river barges, to Jerry's obvious and enthusiastic delight.

My father had pounded three martinis before we even sat down to dinner, that vein making its appearance again in his temple, but he hadn't said a damn word.

I'd been gleeful enough to eat some of my salmon without gagging, too relieved by Dimitri charming Jerry to be pissed that my mother always served Blake's favorites—usually foods I hated—even when he wasn't there.

"You were amazing," I said as we headed down the block to my place. "So amazing. I can't thank you enough."

"You don't need to thank—watch it," he said, taking me by the elbow as I nearly tripped over an uneven part of the pavement. He didn't let go after I steadied, just tucked my hand through his arm and carried on. I could've pulled away. But I didn't. And I didn't want to think too hard about it, either. "You don't need to thank me. I'm glad I didn't fuck up too bad. Thank God my mom made me read so much about Russia when I was a kid. She didn't want me to forget where I came from, since we moved to the US when I was eleven. You know, old enough to remember, but not old enough not to forget if I didn't get reminded about it. Helps that I like to read, I guess. Actually, maybe that's why, because she gave me so many books."

He sounded so open, so casual as he told me about himself in a way he hadn't so far, and I glanced up at him, startled and pleased. He had a half-smile on his lips, and he was looking up at the stars.

"You came here when you were eleven? Not later on? I guess that makes sense. Your accent only comes out sometimes. Is your whole family here?"

He didn't answer right away, and he didn't turn his head to meet my eyes, either. The muscles under my fingers went rigid.

Shit. I'd pushed, and I'd overstepped, and I'd made him uncomfortable.

And why would he want to get into his family history with me, anyway? I was a temporary part of his life. Besides which, he'd seen enough of my family now to know they were as unloving and unlikable as a family could be—not to mention that they were incorrigible snobs, and I already knew Dimitri thought I was, too. Maybe he was even right to an extent.

Did he think I'd make fun of him for having a poor family, or an immigrant family?

I wouldn't. But he might be justified in imagining that I would.

"Some of them are in the States," he said at last. "I'm glad the reading came in handy tonight, is all."

And that was clearly the end of the subject. If I wanted to repay him for the way he'd stepped up to the fancy, gilt-edged plate tonight, so to speak, then I needed to drop it.

Speaking of. "I know I already paid you for all of this, but seriously? That was above and beyond tonight. You didn't have to do more than act respectable. But you charmed the hell out of Jerry, and you even managed not to claw out and take his son-in-law's face off when he wiped his hand on his suit." He really, really had, a moment after shaking Dimitri's. I'd thought I was hallucinating for a second, it was so fucking rude.

Dimitri let out a short, sharp bark of laughter. "I've had worse. Anyway, like you said, you paid me. A lot."

"Still. I feel like you deserve a bonus, or something." We turned off the sidewalk, strolling up the identical brick walkway to my front door. The evening had turned out balmy and beautiful, and the roses in my front yard had started to bloom, perfuming the air and giving the night an almost magical atmosphere. "Is there something you want? I mean, like a present, or something like that? Fancy dinner that we don't have to eat with my parents?"

"You could let me fuck you tonight."

I stopped dead, choked, and started to cough, yanking my hand away from Dimitri's arm to put my hands on my hips. Aaand there went the magic.

"Say fucking what?" I gasped through spasms. "I could *what?*"

Finally getting a handle on it, I straightened up to find him watching me, head cocked, a weird look on his face.

"I'm not getting any anywhere else," he said with a shrug. "After that kind of bullshit, I want to get off. And you're the only option. So if you want to give me a bonus, then bend over. If not, no worries. I'll jerk off in the shower."

Bend over. As simple as that.

Maybe it was for him, since he wouldn't be the one doing it.

A heavy spark of…something bloomed deep in me at the thought of it. Nerves? And speaking of nerves, my whole body thrummed, more aware of him, aware of everything, than it'd been a moment before. Every bit of my exposed skin felt the faint breeze brushing through the yard as if it'd been a high wind, and my clothes rubbed oddly everywhere else.

If not, no worries. He wouldn't pressure me. I didn't have to do it.

But didn't I owe him? I mean, I'd offered anything he wanted. And I got it, I really did. I often wanted a fight or a fuck after I'd had to deal with my family, and their attitude tonight had been even worse than usual—not to mention, Dimitri had really, *really* handled them well.

Nope, I didn't have any choice but to keep my word.

"Okay," I said, my voice a little rough, a little breathy. I'd been coughing, after all. "Yeah. You can fuck me."

The moonlight reflected off of Dimitri's gray eyes, giving them a bright sheen—and over that, they glowed. Silver and gold, molten, mesmerizing.

"Then get inside," he growled. "Before we give the neighbors a show."

He didn't touch me while I hurried up the walkway, trying not to trip over my own feet even though the bricks were perfectly even. And he didn't touch me as I got the door open, carefully took off my shoes—because even in a hurry, hand-stitched Italian leather deserved respect—and started up the stairs, working at the knot of my tie as I did.

But I could still feel him. Through the bond, and through the heat and alpha magic he radiated at my back: a heavy pressure that didn't let me get a full breath, that made my skin crawl with anticipation.

I knew what he felt like inside me now. How his cock would open me up so that his knot could force its way in. Plenty of shifter-centric porn had alpha tops, and I'd seen close-ups of what a knot looked like in someone else's ass: the bottom's hole stretched obscenely, shiny and pink, and his cheeks spread apart, his whole pelvis strained to the limit.

That's what I'd looked like when Dimitri had taken me the other night. That's how I'd look now, with Dimitri watching.

A shuddering moan rose up in my throat, and I choked it back, squeezing my eyes shut against the dizzying humiliation of it. My cock stirred. Nerves. Adrenaline caused physical arousal sometimes. Fear could, too.

I draped my jacket over the chair in my bedroom and tossed my tie on top of it, starting on my shirt buttons.

Dimitri still hadn't touched me and hadn't said a word, simply doing the same with his own clothes, dropping his jacket and then his shirt in the same pile with mine.

Fuck, our clothes. On the same bedroom chair. All mingled

together…the intimacy of it hit me overwhelmingly.

He was my mate.

And my mate had started getting his trousers off, revealing the thick, heavy bulge in the front of his boxers, as if the hard muscles of his chest and shoulders weren't enough to intimidate me. I'd automatically flipped the light switch as I walked into the room, so I could see every detail.

Just like he'd be able to see every detail of me.

I swallowed hard and worked my own zipper open, fumbling my trousers and boxers down and off. Picking up the pants and putting them on the chair was beyond me. I left them where they lay and got on the bed, lying back on the pillows and waiting for Dimitri to tell me how he wanted me. This was his reward, after all. He got to call the shots.

When he stopped on the way to the bed to grab my bespoke trousers off the floor, shake them out, and put them neatly over the back of the chair, the words burst out of me involuntarily: "I can blow you first, if you want."

Oh, Christ. What had I just said? What was wrong with me?

He turned slowly, giving me a fabulous view of his taut back muscles and a hard, muscular ass. Not to mention those legs. It took me a second to scan back up to his face.

"I don't need both," he said. "Your ass is more than enough. You're not into this, right? So that's not fair to ask of you."

He didn't want me to? He didn't *want* me to? Yeah, I didn't want to either, I'd been offering out of generosity, but…fuck that! I had a fucking amazing mouth.

"I'm actually gay, remember? And I'm not a selfish top. I go down on guys I sleep with. It's not a big deal."

His eyes flickered from mine to my mouth, and he reached down, stroking his cock from root to tip, swiping his thumb over the glans. It'd already gotten mostly hard, and it stiffened even more in his grasp. My mouth watered. Jesus, I shouldn't be nervous. I'd sucked plenty of cock.

Maybe I should get on my knees for this? Would he expect that? Having him lie down might be easier, but…and then he took the decision out of my hands, crossing to the bed and climbing up to kneel over me, legs on either side of my hips. The touch of his skin sent a shockwave through me.

"Lean back and open your mouth." That tone of command again, and my mind went all light and distant, my neck hot and prickly.

Dimitri gently took my glasses off my face and set them on the nightstand. I blinked at his blurrier, but still fucking enormous, cock bobbing there a couple of feet from my face.

I leaned back, and he moved up, straddling my waist and bending down to brace a hand on the headboard. The other took hold of his cock and stroked it again, pointing it directly at my mouth.

Porn directors really had something with the camera angle thing. Because from where I was, Dimitri's cock looked like the Washington Monument.

He didn't ask and didn't wait, simply pushing the thick head into my open mouth. It rested heavy on my lower lip, weighed my tongue down, thrust against the roof of my mouth, filling me up, hot and salty and sweet. Dimitri filled my vision, too: the ripple of his hard abs, his torso looming over me.

"Can you take it if I fuck your mouth?"

God, I didn't know. My eyes were watering, my jaw aching already. I'd sucked cock, but never like this, helplessly laid out on my back. And how did he expect me to answer, anyway? I tried to nod, even though I should've been shaking my head, shouldn't I? And I tried to speak, but it came out a garbled moan. My hands flailed, landing on his thighs, fingers digging in frantically.

"I think that's a yes," he said, very low. "I won't go down your throat, Brook."

He thrust, shallowly at first, cock only bumping the back of my mouth, dragging the head over my tongue again and again until I had to move it, teasing the underside of his cock, saliva pooling in the corners of my mouth.

"Fuck, I could come like this. You won't need to spread your legs after all." That almost-growl had me moaning around him, opening my throat to take him deeper even though he'd said I didn't need to.

He thrust again, harder, his other hand wrapping in my hair and tugging my head to an angle that suited him better.

Dimitri could come like this. He could come…and then he wouldn't fuck me. I shoved at his legs, trying desperately to turn my head, suddenly panicked, overwhelmed, my mouth too full and my throat starting to close up—and he pulled out abruptly, fingers still tangled in my hair. He'd tipped my head back, and I blinked up at him, his flushed face and glowing eyes coming into partial focus.

"I promised you a fuck," I gasped. "You're not—you're not the only one who does the job they promised."

A strange, thoughtful expression passed over his face, his jaw tensing. His eyes glittered. "Yeah? You want my knot in your ass, Brook?"

"No! No, I don't want—no! But I *promised*."

"Uh-huh." He still had that odd, considering look on his face, calm even though his hand had tightened in my hair until it hurt. "You did promise. So I should probably make you keep it."

That was all the warning I got before he moved back, released me so that my head thumped down onto the pillows, and took me by the hips, flipping me like I didn't weigh anything at all. My face hit the pillow, another thump, and I yelped and scrabbled at the sheets, trying to get my bearings.

I failed. Dimitri didn't allow me to get a breath, tugging me up with his hands still wrapped around my hips, rubbing his wet cock between the cheeks of my ass. I held myself up the best I could even though my head spun and my lungs labored. The rattle of the nightstand drawer, the click of a cap, and then two slick fingers thrust inside me, fast and hard and dirty.

Before I'd even begun to adjust to that, he'd pulled them out, and his cock took their place, stretching my hole open.

He filled me up in one hard, brutal thrust, punching the last of the air out of my lungs.

He'd gone easy on me before, I realized.

And that was my last coherent thought.

Dimitri pounded me into jelly, cock surging so deep into me with every snap of his hips that I couldn't think, couldn't move, couldn't do anything but take it.

And like before, my body responded. I didn't want to come, I didn't want to…but no matter how hard I bit my lips and clawed my fingers into the mattress, my cock hardened and my balls ached, tight and full.

When he came, he growled long and deep, a feral sound that echoed in my mind and vibrated through my body.

His knot swelled. He thrust it deeper, burying it in me, and he laid one big hand on my ass cheek, pulling me open with his thumb, adding to the stretch and making me whimper.

He'd be seeing me like that, the way I'd pictured, right at this moment. All pink and shiny and swollen, my ass in the air and my thighs spread to relieve the ache of how full I was.

I came like that, helpless to stop it, clenching rhythmically around his knot and practically sobbing into the pillow. My whole body trembled, heart racing.

Dimitri lowered himself down over my limp body and rested his forehead against my shoulder. His hot breath cooled the sweat on my skin and made me shiver.

Neither of us said a word. I couldn't have moved a muscle even if my life depended on it.

At last his knot went down, and he withdrew, the slick pop of his diminished knot coming out of me as loud as a gunshot, it seemed like. I winced and held perfectly still.

"Thanks," Dimitri said. "Fuck. Thank you. I needed that. I'll go shower in my own room, okay? Give you some privacy."

Privacy? After he'd pulled my ass open to watch my body yield to his in the most intimate possible way? I choked down a hysterical laugh that tried to spill out.

"Sure." That was all I could get out. "Okay."

Dimitri hesitated, but then he repeated, "Okay," and got off the bed. The night wasn't cold, but it felt like it once he'd taken away the shelter of his body.

A few rustles told me he'd gathered up his clothes, and then my bedroom door shut behind him. *Thanks. I needed that.* Not exactly a ringing endorsement. If you were hungry, and you got a mediocre sandwich, that might be your reaction. Was that what I was to him? The peanut butter and jelly of fucks? Adequate when you had a physical need?

I'd paid for this.
And apparently I was getting exactly what I'd paid for.

Chapter 11

Come Here

After a decent night's sleep—more than decent, really, I slept better than I had in months or maybe years—I was able to shake off whatever maudlin, self-pitying bullshit I'd allowed myself to wallow in the night before, the result of too much anxiety and adrenaline. Dimitri had knocked Jerry's socks off. My father wouldn't be able to force us to break the bond now that we had that old martinet's approval. Mates were for life, after all.

I'd have to deal with that later, when Dimitri and I did eventually break the bond after I got my position as CEO. But Jerry had to be pushing seventy. He'd have to retire at some point, dammit. We'd make it work.

As I poured my coffee, I found myself actually whistling. It promised to be a beautiful sunny day, and that lifted my spirits even though I'd be spending most of it locked up in a conference room with my sales team.

Fuck it, maybe I'd shift and go for a run after work. Maybe Dimitri would want to join me, and we could check out the waterfall I'd found a ways up in the foothills. I didn't like going all the way out there on my own because of my balance and eyesight issues. In my wolf form, those things weren't much better, although my enhanced hearing and sense of smell compensated a bit. And if I stumbled and sprained or broke something, I'd be in trouble. I might not heal fast enough if I'd fallen down a cliff or into water.

But Dimitri wouldn't let anything happen to me. And it might be fun.

Well, maybe not today—I'd probably have to work late. But soon. As soon as I could get up the courage to ask Dimitri if he wanted to.

He prowled into the kitchen as I was leaning against the counter and sipping my coffee, scrolling through my email on my phone to get a preview of what kinds of crap would be landing on me the second I walked into the office.

I had to laugh when I got a good look at him. In the warm golden glow of the early-morning sun streaming through the kitchen's wide bay window, he redefined seedy: unshaven, boxers crooked, T-shirt on inside-out, overlong hair sticking up wildly in gravity-defying directions.

"Ungh," he said, making a beeline for the coffee. I had to practically jump out of the way to avoid being run over.

"You know, you don't have to get up every morning when I go to work," I said—and I actually meant it, much to my own surprise. I'd always hated it when people slept in. It seemed so lazy. And it made me bitter and jealous, if I were being totally honest. Early rising had been one of my requirements for a mate when I'd made a list a few years back. (With bullet points, obviously, and I made a mental note to find it and burn it before Dimitri ran across it by accident.) Of course, Dimitri wasn't my real mate, so maybe that made all the difference. "It's not like I need you to hold my hand while I have coffee and get dressed. I don't eat big breakfasts, or anything."

Dimitri took a long, loud slurp of his burning-hot black coffee. Ugh, for so many reasons.

But when he turned and half-smiled at me, all big and rumpled and sleep-creased, the picture of friendly morning domesticity, my annoyance melted away instantly.

"Yeah, but you should," he grumbled. "You need to eat more. Anyway, I've got to get used to it. I'm going to start going with you to the office every day, right?"

Right. Jesus, what was wrong with my brain this morning?

"Not today, though. My father still has to give us the official thumbs-up. He will. Jerry liking you backed him into a corner he can't get out of." My face ached with the size of my smile. "That really backfired, inviting Jerry. I think he thought the last-minute summons to dinner would put him in a bad mood and then you'd do the rest. Hoist with his own petard."

Dimitri smiled back, a real one that lit up his eyes. He sipped more of his coffee—quietly this time, thank God. "You're in a good mood this morning."

"Yep. Winning always makes me feel good."

His smile widened into a wicked grin. Why was he looking at me like that? I was allowed to be happy. My father had held the upper hand for twenty-eight years, and for *once* I'd gotten ahead.

"Have a good day at work, Brook," he said after another gulp of coffee. "I'll have dinner ready when you get home if you text me you're on your way."

That put the last bit of shine and polish on my mood, and I was whistling again when I started the car and headed out. Why hadn't I gotten myself a mate a long time ago, if it could be like this?

Murphy's Law probably should've dictated that the rest of the day could only go downhill from there.

But it didn't. My sales team had all their numbers ready, no one argued, and whichever administrative assistant had stocked the executive breakroom that morning had gotten blueberry scones.

And last but not least, my father called me into his office right after lunch, demanded to know why Dimitri hadn't come in to work with me that day, and then dismissed me with a few harsh words about my handling of the Anderson account.

From him, that was the equivalent of flying the white flag.

Life was finally looking up.

***

Walking into the office with Dimitri by my side on Wednesday morning would've been awesome if Jackie, my assistant, hadn't been hovering around very obviously gawking at the show. Her eyes had gone as wide as saucers when the two of us got off the elevator; obviously, somehow, word that I'd gotten myself mated had gone around, and everyone in the building seemed to be popping out of the woodwork to get a look at him in person. There had been a suspiciously large group of employees milling around the lobby downstairs.

When I introduced them, he shook her hand, said hello in that deep, rasping voice of his, and favored her with a devastating smile I hadn't known he had in his arsenal.

I'd never gotten that smile. The hell.

He asked her about her job, smiled some more, and even let a little bit of Russian accent slip through in a way that had her turning all pink and standing way too close to him.

So by the time I managed to chivvy Jackie out and back to her desk, shutting the door firmly behind her, my lingering good mood had faded.

Dimitri strolled around my office, leaning down to peer at a couple of the awards and tchotchkes I had on the shelves next to all the more boring books and files, glancing out the windows, and then turning back to me.

"Nice place," he said. "And nice view."

"Are you referring to the mountains or Jackie?" I asked, with probably unnecessary snideness.

Dimitri's eyebrows went up. "The mountains, but she's pretty too. Something the matter?"

"You're here to make me look good. Not flirt with all the women who work here." I flopped into my chair and opened up my laptop. "Pretending to be into me is kind of part of the job, Dimitri. We're newly mated. Everyone expects us to be all over each other, not already hitting on secretaries like some kind of pathetic fifties cliché."

"Okay," he said slowly, drawing the word out in an incredibly aggravating way. "You want me to come sit on your lap, or something?"

I gaped at him. "No!"

"Okay," he repeated, this time with a shrug, and turned away again, gesturing at the couch and chairs I had on the other side of the room for more casual meetings. "Mind if I sit here, then? Since I have no idea what I'm supposed to be doing. Or I guess I could go hang out with Jackie. She seemed to like me."

That faint ripple of laughter in his voice...was he *mocking* me? Because it sure fucking sounded like it!

"You're here," I said again, through gritted teeth, "to make me look good. So sit there. And look good."

He sat down and shut up, at least. Good? Did he look good? His new black suit definitely did something for him, setting off the way he didn't seem at all like the kind of man who'd wear one. Putting a wolf in a shiny collar didn't make it a lapdog. And Dimitri in a suit exuded more danger than ever.

Of course, it flattered his height and his broad shoulders, the way a good suit always did.

No wonder Jackie had been all over him. Dammit, I liked Jackie. We worked well together. I'd never even noticed her sultry red lipstick and nice ass before today. Now they were all I could think about.

I tried to bury myself in reading through a sales report, but I kept glancing up at Dimitri, who'd pulled out his phone and sprawled into the couch completely at his ease.

A knock on the door heralded Jackie, right on cue.

"I brought coffee for both of you, Brook," she simpered. Well, maybe that was a strong word. But the smile she gave Dimitri as she set his cup down on the table in front of him definitely verged on the unprofessional.

"Thanks," I said sharply. "That's all for now."

With a startled, wounded look in my direction, Jackie hightailed it out of the office and shut the door behind her with force.

Dimitri sighed and shook his head.

"What?" I demanded. "I'm trying to concentrate. She interrupted my train of thought."

"Come here."

"*What?*"

Dimitri put his phone down on the table next to his coffee. "Come. Here."

I was halfway out of my chair before I could muster an angry refusal. My legs carried me around my desk, across the room, and right in front of him.

His expression remained terrifyingly neutral, a blank mask that didn't give me anything at all to work with.

"You don't get to—what the fuck!"

Big hands caught me by the hips and yanked me down into his lap, straddling his thighs, my own legs spread uncomfortably by the wide angle of his.

I opened my mouth to keep arguing, my hands flying up to his shoulders to push myself off of him. And then the words died in my throat as his eyes flared the pure, brilliant gold of the angry alpha. He leaned in, putting his face only an inch from mine.

"Jackie hasn't done anything wrong," he said, voice hard. "She's doing her job. And if she's a little curious about her boss's mate, there's nothing strange about that."

"But she—you—"

"I fucked you two nights ago," he interrupted me. "*You*. Not her." One of his hands shifted, moving down from my hip to cup my ass, fingers tracing the crease. I squirmed in his grip, letting out a hoarse, helpless sound, all my nerves firing at once as every bit of my awareness narrowed down to the brush of his fingers. "I held you down and put my cock in you, I turned you inside out until you came on my knot. *You're* my mate. Remember?"

"Dimitri—"

"Say it, Brook."

My eyes prickled with moisture. The heavy heat in the pit of my stomach kept gathering, as if gravity were stronger there, pushing my body down into Dimitri's lap.

"I'm your mate," I whispered.

His hand tightened, fingers pushing deeper between the cheeks of my ass, caressing my hole through the fabric of my trousers and underwear.

"Yeah, you are. Mine. I'm not looking at Jackie like that. I have a mate. I can fuck you whenever I want, so I don't need her."

The heat of him drew me in further, so that I started swaying into his chest. Maybe gravity *had* gone wonky. Or I'd gotten heavier. Or something.

"You can't fuck me whenever you want. That's—it was a one-time thing." I swallowed hard, my train of thought completely de-railed. His glowing, mesmerizing eyes were so close. Dimitri's body surrounded me. That hand on my ass kept stroking, probing, reminding me of the way he'd owned me the other night.

Dimitri smiled, and it wasn't one of his nice smiles. "Twice, Brook. A two-time thing. And it's going to happen again, isn't it."

That wasn't a question.

Yeah, it would happen again, if he kept touching me like this.

And it wasn't fair of him to take advantage of the mate bond this way. That had to be why I couldn't move, couldn't shake him off and tell him to go fuck himself, because he sure as hell wouldn't be fucking me.

"You're not fucking me again," I said, my voice wavering and a little too high. "You don't even want to. I don't want to," I added, remembering that was the main point I needed to make.

"Whatever you say. But you're my mate, and you should keep it in mind. Stop being a jealous asshole."

That stung, even through the haze of confusion that'd settled over me. "I'm not jealous! Don't be a moron. I'd never be jealous of you."

His eyes went hard, his jaw tense. "Then don't act like it," he said, clipped and cold. "Get up and get back to work, Brook. And stop being a dick to your assistant."

I clambered off his lap stiffly, my muscles not cooperating. He helped me with a shove up by my hips, and the second I'd gotten off of him, he picked up his coffee and his phone and acted like I wasn't even there.

Could I kick him in the shin? That sounded appealing. Or knock him back onto the couch, climb back on his lap, and…

No, the hell. I didn't want to be on his lap. I turned away, so many conflicting impulses swirling around in my brain that I could hardly see straight. For lack of any better ideas, I sat down at my desk and went back to work.

Just like he'd told me to do.

When Jackie knocked at the door an hour later and then waited for me to call out to her to come in, I winced. We really did have a good working relationship. She never interrupted me when I had the door closed unless she needed to, and she always rapped on the door and then opened it immediately, more of a warning so I wouldn't be startled than asking for permission.

"Yeah, Jackie," I said, and the door opened.

"You have that meeting with Adam in ten minutes," she said, sounding formal and subdued. "I cc'd you on the emails about it so you can prep."

I glanced over at Dimitri and found him watching me levelly.

He didn't speak, and his expression stayed neutral, but his emotions leaked through the bond: disappointment, but also…encouragement.

He was on my side. I knew it as surely as I knew my own name. Dimitri had said he was my mate, and now, calmed down and a bit chastened by Jackie's demeanor, I knew I'd been an asshole. Besides, I wasn't jealous! And if my mate bond had me acting like it, I needed to be conscious of it and dial it back.

"Thanks," I said to Jackie, looking her in the eyes and smiling. It felt forced, but she brightened up, so it must have been convincing enough. "I was going to have Dimitri shadow me in that department heads meeting in a while, but he doesn't need to be there while I talk to Adam. Maybe you could show him around a little bit in the meantime?"

Getting the words out took real effort, because sending them off to talk and flirt made me grind my teeth.

But another glance at Dimitri told me it'd been worth it. That incredible, warm, charming smile he'd aimed at Jackie earlier—well, there it was again. Only this time, it was all for me.

"Sure," Jackie chirped, back to her usual cheer. Jesus, I really had been a dick. Tearing my eyes away from my mate took another palpable effort, but at last I did it. Jackie shot me a smile and said, "I'll send Adam in when he gets here. And Dimitri, I'll take you to meet the guys down in engineering. One of them is Russian, I think. Maybe you'd both enjoy saying hi."

She slipped out again after Dimitri thanked her, leaving me feeling like even more of a jerk. Taking him to meet the Russian engineer didn't exactly qualify as trying to get him alone.

And why would she? As I met Dimitri's clear gray eyes again, they penetrated the haze that had descended over me. What had come over me, anyway? And why had he…he'd put me in his lap. I couldn't think about that, about his fingers pressing between my legs, touching my hole. He'd noticed the mate bond fucking with me, and he'd used his position as the dominant mate to break me out of my emotional tangle.

That was all.

A little manipulative, maybe, but I'd also deserved it for acting that way.

"You should take a minute to tell me about this meeting you want me in later," he said, managing to sound genuinely interested. "So I know what you want me to do. Intimidate them? Sit back and keep my mouth shut? Nod and agree with everything you say?"

My immediate impulse was to tell him to simply sit back and keep his mouth shut—which, to be fair, would probably be intimidating enough. That had been my basic plan for having him around, so I hadn't bothered briefing him for the meeting.

But now that he mentioned it…maybe if he really wanted to help me, and not simply be a silent prop in my unspoken war with my father, he could be genuinely useful. Two of the other alpha-douchebag VPs who'd be in this meeting took every opportunity to undermine me: stealing my ideas, talking behind my back, and sucking up to my father. I knew anything I suggested in this meeting, which was meant to help us keep our respective departments communicating and collaborating, would get shot down. And then probably resurrected later on, when one of those assholes emailed the more senior executives with "his" bright ideas.

"Sit back and keep your mouth shut at first," I said after considering it for a moment. "You can feel free to look as unfriendly and threatening as you want, though. You know the expression I'm talking about." He raised his eyebrows at me and then scowled, fangs very slightly on display, and I cracked up. "Yeah, like that. I'll present my ideas at some point. They'll ignore them and suggest their own. Then you can tell them their ideas suck and suggest *your* own, which will just be mine, only in your own words. And we'll see how that goes. Okay?"

Dimitri's eyebrows went up even higher. "Sure, I can do that. But you know your company culture sucks, right? This is such bullshit. Who cares whose idea it is as long as it's a good one?"

"Yeah," I sighed. "Welcome to the corporate world. Honestly, it's not that different from other places, I don't think, except that here it's all based on who's an alpha. But it's the same shitty politics everywhere."

"God save me from having your job," he muttered. "Seriously, if you were worried I might try to cut you out? Don't be."

"Even if it came with my salary?"

Dimitri laughed, stood up, and slipped his phone in his pocket, picking up the jacket he'd shrugged out of at some point while I worked. "I'm your kept mate, Brook. I get your salary without having to do your job. I don't have any interest in rocking the boat."

Amusement, warmth, and sincerity trickled through the bond, reassuring me and making me feel better than I had all morning.

When Jackie announced Adam, and she and Dimitri went off for their tour, that sensation lingered, keeping me upbeat, confident, and ready to take on the world.

Chapter 12

Twice Is a Coincidence

After that first day in the office, Dimitri and I settled into a routine. We left for work together three or four days a week, with him staying home and doing his own thing the other days. On weekends I stuck to my usual system: wake up early, go for a run, and work from home.

He told me my life sucked, but he didn't try to stop me. And occasionally he'd even join me for the runs, both of us shifting into our wolf forms and racing through the woods until we were panting and exhausted. I liked those mornings. Company without any expectation of conversation soothed me after full weeks of nothing but talking, negotiating, telling people what to do.

Dimitri had kicked ass in that first meeting, doing exactly what I'd asked of him and pulling it off flawlessly. No passive-aggressive emails with my stolen ideas. No arguing.

Although the fact that it'd worked, that my colleagues listened to him when they wouldn't to me simply because his dick had a knot...well, that rankled. Deeply.

Even though I'd known it'd be that way.

I had to keep reminding myself that it wasn't Dimitri's fault; it was theirs. Sometimes I started to resent him for the way he forced my plans through in meetings when he knew jack shit about what we were doing or why.

But I'd paid him for exactly that. My father had put this company culture in place, and Dimitri was helping me get to a position where I could start to undo it. Being angry with him would be both unfair and counterproductive.

Still, the stress had started to get to me, and to make it worse, my mother had gotten the bit between her teeth regarding a formal mating reception a day or two after my father had let go of the idea of forcing me to break my bond with Dimitri. She'd finally reached the point in planning where she wanted to harass me every ten minutes.

"And of course the club had to have that kitchen fire last week, so I've had to arrange outside catering at the last minute." Jesus. As if the club's management had planned the fire merely for her inconvenience. Her voice hadn't lost any of its strident insistence for being filtered through my car's speakers, though the asshole honking at someone who'd cut him off in six o'clock rush hour traffic in front of me definitely made her harder to hear. It was nearly a month after Dimitri had gone to work with me for the first time, and one of the days he'd opted to stay home. At least he didn't have to listen to this.

"In any case," she went on, "that's arranged now. But I need you to step up and take an interest, Brook. It wasn't necessary to send them invitations because they're not part of the main guest list, but I do need to know which of...Dimitri's...family—" She always paused before and after his name, as if trying to remember it. It made my jaw clench until my molars hurt, and I was doubly, triply glad I didn't have him in the car with me. "—will be attending, and where they'll be staying. And how much attention they'll require. I'd like to spend as little time as possible in their company. I can't imagine that they'd be presentable."

I had to slam on the brakes as someone ahead of me changed lanes with more enthusiasm than attention, and it took me a second to catch up to that.

When I did, my blood ran cold. I hadn't even thought about the fact that my family would expect his to be there. And I had no idea where they were, who they were, how many there were, or if they were even alive.

I was so fucking screwed.

"Are you listening to me, Brook?" she demanded. "You need to tell me how many allowances we'll need to make. I don't want to be humiliated."

"They'll—um. Fuck." Fuck, fuck, *fuck*.

"Brook!"

I winced. "Sorry, I—wasn't talking to you." I'd been talking to myself *about* her, but details. "Someone cut me off. I'm driving."

"Then pull over and give me your full attention. Better yet, you can come here as soon as you—"

Oh, shit, no. Please no. "No! No, I'm paying attention. I'll talk to Dimitri about his family. They may not be able to make it. Then it wouldn't be an issue."

Let her drop it, please let her drop it...

"It would absolutely be an issue," she said, and my blood went from cold to icy. "If we introduce your mate to our friends and your father's colleagues without any of his family present, it'll be a disaster. Surely you understand how important it is for some of them to attend." A pause. "The less objectionable ones. No doubt you can find someone in his family tree who isn't entirely unsuitable."

She sounded like she had a lot of doubts about it.

I had literally never, in a lifetime of disliking most of my relatives, been quite so ashamed of being one of them. Yes, I'd had the same thoughts about Dimitri when I met him. But those had been—practical. He had to sell a certain image to my parents.

Who wanted to sell a certain image to their friends.

Yeah, maybe not so different after all.

Self-knowledge could be such a bitch.

"I'll talk to him. If they're not familiar with events like this, I'll make sure I help them with formal clothing and everything." I'd be doing that in any case, but not for my family's benefit; if any of Dimitri's family did want to come, I'd do my best to make up for having been an asshole in my own mind by helping them get ready for it for their own comfort. Feeling out of place at something like that was the worst.

And I should know. I'd been born and bred for it, trained for it, always dressed perfectly for it, and I still never managed to be at ease.

But how the hell was I supposed to tell Dimitri that his family, whoever and wherever they were, would be expected at this fucking reception? With almost no notice?

"I suppose I'll need to leave that aspect of this in your hands," she said, sounding more dubious than ever. "You do have a good eye for style, Brook. On that note, you'll be glad to hear that the linens..."

I had to split my focus between her dissertation on cream versus ivory and the traffic, which continued to be heavier than usual—my remaining focus, anyway. Most of my brain had gotten stuck on the idea of broaching this subject when I got home. It was a long, hot, loud, miserable drive home, with my mind spinning in frantic circles, and by the time I got her off the phone and pulled into my driveway, I'd had it.

Completely.

I stomped into the house and slammed the door behind me, aware that I was acting like a toddler and barely able to care.

The house didn't smell like food.

And when I got my shoes off and went into the living room, I found Dimitri sprawled on the couch, totally at his ease.

"Jesus, if you're going to let me deal with those assholes by myself all day, you could at least cook!"

"My day was fine, thank you," Dimitri said, swinging his legs off the couch and setting the book he'd been reading face-down on the coffee table to keep his place. It didn't look like one of mine, or I'd have snapped his head off for treating it that way. "How was yours? No, don't answer that. You're one email away from a total meltdown, aren't you?"

"I don't have meltdowns!" That came out a bit less emphatic than I'd wanted, the wind taken out of my sails by his calm demeanor. "Anyway, I'm hungry."

Dimitri rolled his eyes and got up. "You're not really making much of a case for yourself. I'll heat something up. But I told you the deal: you text me when you're leaving, I'll have dinner ready. You didn't text. I'm not going to sit here with the food getting cold until nine, Brook."

On that last bit, he actually sounded…peevish? Oh, Christ.

"Dimitri, are we having our first real mate fight?"

"We're not fighting. I'm telling you how it is." He turned and headed for the kitchen, leaving me gaping after him without any retort whatsoever.

Kind of hard to argue with someone who not only made your food, but also outweighed you by enough to squish you into the floor.

Getting some dinner knocked me out of my strop a little bit, but not enough to want to discuss the mating reception. Surely I could pawn my mother off with some excuse. But would Dimitri be offended if I didn't even ask? Had he been expecting me to?

I toyed with the last few bites of mashed potatoes on my plate, staring down at the patterns my fork made.

"Okay, you need to do something about your attitude," Dimitri said, startling me into glancing up.

"My attitude's fine." He just looked at me without saying a word. "Okay, my attitude sucked earlier, and I'm sorry. I'm tense. I shouldn't have snapped at you."

"I can take it." He shrugged. "Apology accepted. But you need to relax. Maybe you need to get laid."

The fork dropped out of my nerveless fingers, clattering on the plate. "Get what?"

"Laid, Brook. Sex. You know, you have an orgasm, you release some tension, you feel better."

"But I can't sleep with anyone but you, so getting laid won't help me," I said without thinking, and then winced when his expression darkened, his eyes glowing faintly. Shit. That had been really rude. True, of course, because I didn't like getting fucked. But still rude.

"Won't help you how, exactly?" he asked, his tone low and dangerous. "Because you got off just fine when we fucked before."

"No, I didn't—I mean, there was some—that was a fluke!" My heart beat so fast it vibrated in my fingertips. "The formation of the mating bond made me—it was unexpected."

Dimitri's eyes brightened, the glow keeping me fixed in place like prey. "We weren't mating the second time. So two flukes, you mean. Twice is a coincidence, is that what you're saying?"

It *had* been a coincidence, obviously, and I couldn't believe he'd be such a dick about it. "It was a fluke," I repeated. "I'm not into getting knotted. It was something about the circumstances. Or something like that. Anyway, it's not stress relief for me."

The very slight lifting of the corners of Dimitri's mouth, and the gleam of fang it showed me, raised all my hackles. How dare he laugh at me!

"Okay. I knotted you, and you got off on it. I knotted you again, and you got off on it. Again. That's no fluke. But I'm not going to argue with you about it."

He wasn't going to—what did he think he was doing? He didn't believe me, and I *hated* it when people didn't believe me. Besides, it wasn't like he had any moral high ground!

"And what about you? You're straight, right? No interest in men at all. But this is the second time you've wanted to fuck me when you didn't need to."

His smile widened into a grin, and my heart sank.

"Unlike you, I can admit it when I enjoyed something. Yeah, it got me off. A tight hole will do that. Fucking you is kind of adjacent to what I usually enjoy." He leaned forward, obviously about to go for the jugular. "What's your excuse?"

"I don't have—I don't need—" I stammered into silence, face hot and scalp prickling with frustration. "I don't need an excuse, because it was a fluke!"

"Uh-huh. But we don't need to fuck." He got up, collecting both of our plates and heading for the sink. "I'm fine jerking off. You're the one who's so tense you're about to snap. Again."

I stared at his broad back as he started rinsing the dishes, almost surprised smoke wasn't rising from his shirt from the force of my glare.

So tense I was about to snap? I needed to get laid? Where the hell did he get off? If he fucked me again, there was no way I'd come. And his ego needed puncturing. Did he think he was God's gift to anyone who spread their legs for him, or something? It'd be so goddamn satisfying to lie back, all bored and limp, and let him go to town on me without me getting anything out of it. Show him that his knot wasn't all that, after all.

"Fine. We'll fuck," I said tightly. "And then after I don't enjoy it, you'll admit I was right."

Dimitri went still for a second, so briefly I almost thought I'd imagined it, and then went right back to washing the dishes.

"Go upstairs and get ready, then," he said. "I'll be there in a minute. I need to earn my kept-mate keep."

Wait, wasn't he going to crow about it? Trash-talk me, or

something? Tell me how he was going to make me scream?

But then guilt smote me, even through my anger and confusion. "You know you don't have to do all the chores, right? I can load the dishwasher. I didn't pay you to be my maid, Dimitri. I mean, wasn't the actual housecleaner here this morning?"

"She's not here now," he said mildly. "I really don't mind. Go upstairs. Seriously."

After a moment's hesitation, I got up and left the kitchen, more confused than ever. Before Dimitri, I'd literally never seen an alpha do anything that could be construed as domestic labor. Was that my family and pack's shitty attitudes about preserving the proper social hierarchy, or was it a function of being a rich kid whose family didn't do a ton of domestic labor, period? It wasn't like my mother washed her own dishes either, after all. I only knew how to take care of myself in some basic way because I hadn't bothered to use my allowance to pay for someone to do it for me while I was away at college.

Christ, Dimitri had me all turned around and upside-down.

But the one thing I did know for sure, was: He obviously didn't really want to fuck me that much, if it could wait, as far as he was concerned, until the dishes were done and the kitchen cleaned up. I was a convenient hole for him, nothing more. And not even a particularly appealing one at that, apparently.

All right. My pride was truly on the line now. There was no way I'd let him win this one.

I stripped down and got in the shower, hissing in pleasure as the hot water beat down on my hard-as-rocks shoulder muscles. Dimitri did have a point about needing to relax. Maybe I should ask my mother where she went for her spa days.

My hair shampooed, I reached for the soap—and inspiration struck.

I could cheat. If I got off before he even touched me... My cock, half-hard since we'd started talking about having sex—and I really had been neglecting my body's needs lately, clearly, if talking about Dimitri fucking me could have that effect—gave a hopeful twitch.

That would be contrary to the spirit of proving Dimitri wrong, wouldn't it? And yet...it wasn't like we'd made any kind of agreement about the terms. It wasn't cheating if there weren't any rules.

My hand wrapped around my cock, and I bit back a groan as heat lanced through me, from the base of my cock to my balls and into the center of me. Christ, I didn't usually have such a hair-trigger.

It only took a couple of minutes of stroking myself off, biting my lips to keep in any betraying sounds that Dimitri's alpha ears might've picked up, before I was right on the edge.

My ass clenched around nothing. Without thinking about it, I reached around behind myself, soapy fingers slipping into the crack of my ass, ready to push inside and—I jerked my hand away, cursing, curling it into a fist.

No. No, I didn't need a fucking finger in my ass to come. I didn't need anything in my ass, big and thick and hot, shoving me open and taking me apart...

The moan I'd been suppressing tore out of my throat as my orgasm burst out of my cock, painting the tiles and dripping down over my fingers. I slumped against the wall of the shower, chest heaving, the world swimming around me.

Okay. That had been weird. But I'd gotten myself off, so mission accomplished. Dimitri wouldn't stand a chance.

But now I needed to put my fingers in my ass after all to make sure I'd gotten all clean. Well, I had a good reason. I should've thought of that before. Two fingers were a tight fit, but they'd get me cleaner. My breath started coming faster again. I twisted them, probing all around, my balls starting to get all heavy and tight again.

Fuck. I pulled my fingers out and turned around, spreading my cheeks and rinsing thoroughly. The water beat down on my hole, too light, too much of a tease.

There. Clean. Dimitri wouldn't make me come. I had willpower, dammit. And my pride. And a point to make.

I didn't want him any more than he wanted me.

Chapter 13

No Rules

Dimitri thumped up the stairs a minute after I'd settled myself on the bed to let the last of the dampness from the shower evaporate and scroll through the emails that'd come in since I left the office.

Again, not cheating. If guys could recite baseball statistics while they fucked in order to hold off an orgasm, surely I could use the sales team's complaints about their commission structure to get myself not in the mood.

The half-open door creaked as he pushed it wide. I glanced up in time to catch him tilting his head, scenting the air.

"You jerked off in the shower," he said. "That's cheating."

Dammit.

But I wasn't going to let him throw me off my game. "There's no cheating if there weren't any rules," I said loftily.

That earned me a slowly-growing smile that became a terrifyingly predatory grin as he advanced on the bed. He moved slowly, too, enough that it made me want to scream. Dimitri's shirt came off, whipped over his head and tossed carelessly aside, and he had his jeans unbuttoned by the time he made it to the side of the bed.

Since it seemed like the time for coyness had fled, I hadn't bothered putting any of the covers over me, simply sprawling out naked.

And as he started to shove his jeans down and I got a glimpse of that big, alpha cock, my heart started to race—and my own cock started to fill again. If Dimitri saw that, I'd be so screwed, and not only in the way I expected to be. I started to flip over onto my stomach, and to my horror, Dimitri lunged forward, grabbing me by the hips and pinning me to the bed.

"Stay on your back." His eyes glowed down at me, emphasizing the command in his voice. "We're doing it like this tonight."

"I'd be more comfortable—"

"You want me to tie you down, or are you going to do what I tell you?"

My chest clenched into a knot, and further down...fuck, fuck, *fuck*. No, I did *not* want him to tie me down. But I couldn't stay on my back, either. He'd be able to see everything. My body's perfectly natural reaction to being nervous. And he'd misinterpret all of it.

In desperation, I said, "You don't want me on my back, okay? You'll see that I'm a guy. You can kind of pretend when I'm face down, but not like this. How are you going to make your point if you can't get it up?"

"I'm getting it up right now." He let go of me to get his jeans and boxers the rest of the way off, and I could see that indeed he was. I swallowed hard, trying to get some moisture into my dry throat. "Don't worry about me," Dimitri continued, his voice a low, dangerous purr. "I'll fuck you just fine, Brook. All you have to do is not enjoy it."

Fine. I could do that on my back as well as on my stomach. Dimitri could see how much he enjoyed working with a totally unresponsive man, with a man's body and no interest in getting fucked.

When he got on the bed, nudging my legs apart with his knees, I didn't react; I simply lay there, arms at my sides, head on the pillows, letting him adjust me however he wanted. The rough hair on his legs tickled my inner thighs.

Dimitri cocked his head, staring down at me like a logic problem that needed solving.

"How often does anyone touch you, Brook?"

"You know I haven't gotten laid in a while," I snapped, nervous and ill at ease and wishing I knew where the hell he was going with this so I could prepare to counter it.

He reached down and traced his fingers over my ribs, so lightly it made me shiver. "That's not what I meant."

More gentle strokes, with his fingertips only: across to the other side and along my ribs there, up to my chest, tracing the curves of my pecs but avoiding my nipples. And then down, along my sternum and circling my navel. Everywhere he touched me, my skin came to life, tingling even after he'd moved on. It felt like it should be visible, my body changed in his wake. Glowing, maybe, the same gold that shone out of his eyes as he watched his hand on my skin.

My breath had started coming faster, my chest rising and falling rapidly.

Dimitri took his hand away and leaned down, bracing himself on either side of my head.

He was almost close enough to kiss me. Those eyes with their gorgeous flecks, like moss on granite, filled my vision completely.

And now all I could think about was his lips on mine.

As if he'd read my mind, he whispered, "You kiss guys, right? When you used to fuck them."

When I used to fuck them? Of course, I didn't anymore, not now that I'd mated.

But he made it sound so permanent.

I had to swallow before I could say, "Yeah. I kiss guys. But you're not gay. You don't want to kiss me."

Something flickered in those beautiful eyes, there and gone again. "Sure, I guess I don't," he said, and shifted down, his breath hot on my chin and my neck.

A kiss would've thrown me for a loop, but this was worse, somehow, the way he leaned down so slowly, his long hair brushing my lips and my jaw, and pressed his mouth to my chest.

So softly. Barely there. Hot and with a flick of his tongue. And then down, tasting my skin and finding one nipple, catching it between his lips.

Not reacting to that wasn't an option. I arched up, a moan wavering out of me. And then another, higher and ending in a whimper, as he pulled my nipple into his mouth and suckled me, his tongue swirling around and around, tight suction arrowing straight down to my cock.

When he released me, he blew on my wet flesh, hot and cold and too much on my oversensitized skin.

His tongue trailed across my chest. Oh, Christ, he meant to go for the other one.

"Don't," I gasped. "Don't, it's—please."

Dimitri lifted his head, pinning me with those eyes. "You mean it's turning you on?"

"It's not fair," I whispered.

"There's no cheating if there weren't any rules," he growled, and dipped his head to suck the other nipple into his mouth.

My cock brushed his abdomen where he'd leaned down close, and I realized it'd gotten all the way hard again, straining up and begging for attention.

Dimitri chuckled, the vibration going right into me, and released my nipple with an obscene pop. He didn't say anything. He didn't need to. I'd already lost, and he hadn't even opened me up yet. Dimitri was going to make me come on his cock like a slut. I might come before he fucked me at this rate.

He worked his way down, kissing and licking, setting me on fire.

But all that pleasure wasn't mine. Part of it trickled through the bond, showing me an echo of my own need.

"You want me," I choked out as he nibbled my hipbone, hair brushing over my abdomen. "You really want me."

He glanced up sharply. "I like to win just as much as you do, Brook."

That deflated me like a pricked balloon, and I had to squeeze my eyes shut against the moisture that gathered there.

But it didn't do anything about the gathering storm inside me, pressure demanding a release. The humiliation of it nearly took my breath away, but when he brushed his hand over my cock, I still pressed up into the touch, trying and failing to bite back a moan.

I didn't expect him to suck me off, obviously, but it was a shock when he kept going, kissing down my thigh. I'd thought he'd stop at my hips.

But he hadn't, and when his big hands pressed my thighs wide and his head kept moving down, it startled me enough to open my eyes and lift my head to stare down at him.

"What are you doing?" My voice came out all raspy and wrecked. "What—you're straight."

He shrugged, jostling my legs with his broad shoulders. Jesus, he had me opened up wide to fit him. I was a normal sized guy, but he made me look delicate, spread out like that with his huge body in between my legs.

"Yeah, I'm straight. But I've fucked women up the ass. Remember? And going down on that part of a woman's not that different."

Before I could begin to process what that meant, he lowered his head, lifted my balls out of the way with one hand, and pressed his tongue to my hole.

Nerve endings I hadn't realized I had lit up like firecrackers, every swipe and wriggle of that hot, wet, muscular tongue of his sending shockwaves into my balls and cock and up my spine, until the top of my head felt like it might explode. My eyes rolled back in my head as he thrust his tongue into me, stabbing it inside my body and stretching the rim of my hole.

No one had ever done this to me. For me? Definitely *to* me, because Dimitri was in charge and in control, forcing me open, until the pressure in my chest built unbearably and I threw my head back and cried out helplessly, a garbled mixture of no words at all and, horribly, his name. My hands flew up and tangled in his hair of their own volition. I had to hang on to something, and my fingers wrapped in the thick strands, tangling and tugging.

"You going to come like this, Brook?" he asked, muffled against my flesh. He nipped me, quick and hard enough to make me yelp, the edge of my hole stinging and throbbing. A hot swipe of his tongue soothed the pain and had me nearly sobbing with the pleasure of it. "You love getting your ass played with. You're such a fucking liar. Top, my ass."

Oh, God, if only I'd had the wherewithal to deliver one of the obvious comebacks to that. But I didn't, and he was going to make me come, and I let go of his hair with my right hand and wrapped it around my aching cock, because I had to come *now*, I had to, and it only took two quick, hard strokes with Dimitri's mouth on me, sucking hard on my swollen flesh.

Hot spurts hit my stomach and chest and spilled down over my hand, all my muscles seized up, and I tried to keep in a groan but ended up letting out a high, keening cry instead.

When I got my eyes open, panting and trembling all over from the aftershocks, Dimitri had sat up on his heels and was staring down at me, eyes wide and glowing.

"Look me in the eye and say the word 'fluke' again," he said hoarsely. "Come on. I fucking dare you."

I blinked up at him, too dazed to even be angry. But my brain had come back online, partially at least, enough for me to see the flaw in his reasoning.

"You didn't knot me. That's the part that was supposed to make me come. So it doesn't count."

Dimitri's eyes narrowed, and he leaned down in a way that would've had me shrinking back to escape if I'd had anywhere to go. My head pressed down into the pillows, but that was as far as I could get.

"You know, that sounds a lot like you trying to talk me into knotting you anyway. And you know what? I'm hard. I need a fuck too. So I'm going to." He bared his teeth at me, and I flinched. He laughed and added, "And you're going to come again when I do."

"I'm not," I protested weakly as he sat up and grabbed the lube out of my nightstand. "No way. Not a third time. And I don't like it anyway."

"Okay." His mild, indifferent tone set my alarm bells ringing and had me all tense again in an instant. "Fine. So here's what we're going to do." He popped the cap on the lube and poured a generous amount over his fingers. "I'm going to open you up." I couldn't tear my eyes away from his long, slick fingers as he lowered his hand to my hole. "And then I'm going to fuck you." Two of those fingers were rubbing my hole, now, pushing inside slightly deeper on every pass. "And then I'm going to knot you." Both fingers shoved in all at once, and I squirmed and bit my lips, refusing to give him the satisfaction of more moans. "And the whole time, you're going to tell me how it feels. You know, how much you hate it."

"I'm not going to—ohh," I moaned at last, because he'd crooked his fingers, and it felt like he'd electrified me. "I'm not going to do that!"

Dimitri twisted his hand and went even deeper, all the way to the last knuckle. "Yeah, you are. Tell me, Brook. Say it. Tell me you don't like this at all."

"I don't—Dimitri, I can't—" *I can't let you win. I can't lie convincingly when you're inside me. I can't give you what you want from me, because I'll never be able to look at myself in the mirror again.* "Oh," I panted, as he finger-fucked me in a hard, deep rhythm. "Oh, God. That feels—terrible."

"Yeah?" He smiled down at me, eyes fixed on my flushed, wide-eyed face. "What's the worst part?"

I couldn't, I couldn't…but I had to, because he'd told me to, and I didn't seem to be able to resist him.

"Your fingers are so big," I gasped. "So—so fucking big." I had to spread my legs as wide as I could to push down on them, to try to relieve the discomfort, the ache, that'd taken over my lower body. "It's like you're turning me inside out."

Dimitri let out a harsh, wordless sound and tugged them out of me. "I'll have to give you something bigger, then." He wrapped his slick hand around his cock and stroked it, spreading lube from the base to the already-gleaming head. "So you have something to really complain about."

That startled a choked laugh out of me, and before I managed to answer, he'd grabbed me by the hips, tilted me up, and thrust inside. He filled me so completely he knocked the breath and the words right out of me, and I writhed there for a moment, impaled and stuffed.

"Tell me," he growled, leaning down and nuzzling my ear.

"So much bigger." He thrust again, and my arms flew up to cling to his back, trying to find some equilibrium as I adjusted to his cock buried in me. How did it feel even bigger when he took me like this instead of on my hands and knees? "Are all alphas this big?"

Those words had slipped past my lips without my conscious permission, and I wished I could swallow them back down when Dimitri outright laughed, never pausing in his slow, deep thrusts.

"I have no idea. You thinking of going comparison shopping?"

My arms tightened around his broad back. "No, of course not! I wouldn't want—I don't like being fucked." He worked a hand under my ass and lifted me higher, slamming his cock home and hitting me right where it counted. Stars danced in my blurring vision, and I clung to him, fingers digging into his skin. "I hate this," I moaned. "Hate—every—oh, fuck, Dimitri, *please*—"

"I'll give you what you need. What you don't want," he panted, his mouth against the side of my throat. I turned my head to bare myself to him, and he sucked on my skin, letting his mouthful go to add, "I'll put my knot in you so deep you'll never think about any other alpha."

"I don't want any other alpha." Another slam of his hips, harder this time, hard enough to fold me almost in half, and I screamed, so close, needing…only what had I said? I didn't mean that, I meant—"I don't want any alpha, I don't want to be knotted, please, harder, please…"

I couldn't control myself anymore, and the words spilling from my mouth made me writhe in shame, but they kept coming. More pleas and moans, his name, all jumbled together.

Dimitri gave me what I begged for, fucking me until the headboard slammed into the wall and the mattress screamed as loud as me, until all I could feel was his cock in my reamed-out hole and his mouth working over my throat.

My fangs started to drop, my claws itching at my fingertips, and I knew I'd be drawing blood on his back, but I couldn't stop it—and then he came inside me, his knot growing, forcing me open, pressing so hard on all of my inner flesh that it was too much, too much, too—

Another scream wrenched out of my raw throat, and my muscles went rigid, clamping down on him as a third, impossible orgasm caught me in its grip and flipped the world upside-down around me. I hadn't even been hard. It didn't seem to matter. Everything whirled around me, or I was spinning, and I fell back into the bed, my arms sliding off Dimitri's back and flopping down beside me.

Reality came back slowly: the weight of Dimitri's body pinning me down, the deep, perfect ache inside where he still had me filled to capacity, his tongue, tracing lazy, soothing strokes on the bruises he'd left on my throat. His long hair tickling the side of my face. Sticky wetness absolutely everywhere, in me and on me. The bond humming contentedly, replete with satisfaction from both sides of it.

I didn't hate anything about this. And I hadn't hated any of what brought me here.

The thought of how smug Dimitri would be drained away some of my afterglow, but it wasn't enough to make me move.

"You taste really good," he said at last. "Everywhere." He licked me again. "So soft."

"I'm not soft." I'd meant to be definite about that, but it came out sounding more like, *Lick me again.*

Dimitri hummed, licked me again, and then pressed a soft kiss to the throbbing spot where he'd sucked on me the most before dropping his head down onto the pillow next to mine. "Not every-where. Some places. You taste good where you're not soft, too." A pause. "I won, by the way."

Aaand there it was.

I had to make one last effort to recover some of my dignity. "You can have three flukes in a row."

"You referring to the three times I knotted you and you came like crazy, or the three times you came just tonight?"

My face burned. Check-fucking-mate, and I couldn't help laughing. "You're such an asshole."

"Yeah." He lifted his head and craned his neck, peering down into my face. The slight smile hovering on his lips could've been in-terpreted as smug, but…that light in his eyes. "Next time, we'll make it four flukes in a row. Whichever way you take that, I'm okay with making it happen. Part of my job, right?"

Part of his job.

Right. Because I'd paid him for this, and he was making the best of it.

"Sure," I managed. "Let's sleep for a while, okay?"

He gave me a funny look, like he knew damn well I was desper-ate to change the subject, but he only said, "Sure, Brook," and settled down again, his head next to mine.

I lay there staring at the ceiling, Dimitri on top of me and all around me, the heavy warmth of his body, his citrusy alpha scent, the bond woven around us both. I'd thought paying for a mate would avoid unnecessary complications. That it'd make sure I could get what I wanted and then move on.

Christ. I'd really miscalculated. And denial only went so far; I'd hit the end of the road.

Whether it was the mate bond influencing me—and I knew, I *knew*, rationally, that bonds didn't really work like that—or some flaw, some weakness in me, or simply Dimitri himself, all the good qualities I'd never expected him to have, the way he'd given me what I'd never known I wanted…well, I wouldn't be moving on. Not easily, anyway.

And that made the prospect of getting what I wanted, and thus getting Dimitri out of my life, a lot less appealing.

I wanted to put my arms around him. Touch him, feel the texture of his skin, soak in as much of his heat as possible.

He wouldn't welcome that.

So I lay there with my arms at my sides and closed my eyes, determined to get myself under control even though my chest had a hollow, echoing space in it that made me sick and shaky.

I had a plan for my life. I'd stick to that. What choice did I have?

Chapter 14

Family

Dimitri went to work with me the next day, imposing in his sharp suit and towering over me as he followed me into my first meeting, a presentation to the board about my strategy for my department.

Having him at my back felt...not comforting, because I was a professional, and I didn't need to be comforted at work. Emotions weren't my primary mode there. But it did give me the confidence you could only really get from having someone, well, at your back. Supporting you in anything you did, and making sure you knew that no matter what, there was at least one person in the room who wouldn't dismiss you.

When had I started counting on Dimitri to be there to support me rather than being annoyed that I needed him in the first place?

Maybe around the same time I'd started looking forward to coming home from work on those days he didn't go with me, knowing that my house wouldn't be cold and empty and lonely, with nothing to eat and no one to talk to and no reason to do anything but keep working.

"The two of you make a good team," one of our most annoying board members told me as we walked out of the conference room. He favored me with a condescending smirk. "His influence has really improved the quality of your presentations."

Okay, so *that* rankled, and I glared at his retreating back as he sauntered off to do whatever board members did when they weren't terrorizing junior executives. Stare in the mirror and congratulate himself on being so awesome, maybe? Asshole. My presentation had actually been almost precisely the same the last time I'd tried to give it, only this time, I'd had an alpha sitting there nodding along.

I felt Dimitri behind me before he spoke, a whiff of his scent and the heat of him wrapping around me.

"You think next time you should put a life-size photo of my knot in the middle of your slide deck to make it even better?" he grumbled in my ear. "Asshole."

And just like that, my fury evaporated. Even a stopped clock was right twice a day; Dimitri and I did make a good team, only not the way that prick thought we did. It wasn't his omnipotent alphaness making me better. It was the two of us working together to manipulate assholes like the ones on the board into doing what I wanted them to do.

It gave me the courage to bring up the issue of Dimitri's family and my mother's demands about the mating reception, although I waited until we were in the car on the way home, cruising along in moderate traffic and with a comfortable silence between us.

Dimitri leaned back, sighed, and yanked at his tie, loosening it until he could pull it over his head and fling it into the back seat.

The first time he'd done that I'd expostulated with him about treating silk that way.

Now it only made me smile.

My belly clenched, heavy and cold. God, what was I going to do when he left me?

For that matter, what was *he* going to do? Maybe I could ask him to stick around for a while. Give him that stipend he'd mentioned. Would he be willing to stay if I paid him?

That cold, weighty sensation only intensified at the thought.

Paying a man I didn't know to mate with me for a clearly defined purpose and with a clearly defined end date might not be the most dignified course of action, but I'd been able to live with it. Paying *Dimitri*, the man I now knew and—liked, to be my mate on a continuing, open-ended basis? That was different. It meant I'd be paying him to fuck me. Paying him to pretend to enjoy it as more than a stopgap while he couldn't have a relationship, or a sexual partner, he truly wanted. To act like he wanted *me*.

It'd mean admitting to myself, and by default to him, that I truly was too pathetic and undesirable to attract anyone on my own merits.

We'd stopped at a red light, and I glanced at him out of the corner of my eye. My glasses left me with shitty peripheral vision, but

I could still make out the harsh lines of his profile, the prominent nose and strong jaw. The faint smile on his lips, the breadth of his shoulders filling all the space allowed by the passenger seat and then some. His legs sprawled out in front of him, long and muscular.

I didn't need to think about it, let alone broach the subject, right now. Later. I could put that off.

But the conversation about the mating reception had to happen.

I drew in a deep breath. "My mother's been getting things ready for that big party she's giving for our mating," I said. "She's been on my case about it."

"Sure," Dimitri replied easily, as if I hadn't just handed him the equivalent of a social death sentence. "You told me that was coming up. You're the boss, Brook. Tell me what to do and where to go, and I'll have your back."

His immediate willingness to help me however he needed to should've warmed me, dissipated the chill in my chest, but that reminder that he was willing because I'd employed him to be...I bit my lip and forced it down. No. Not now.

"It's not just you, though." Okay, I had to do this. He'd react badly. But I didn't have a choice. "She wants your family there. I guess she was assuming that we'd already given them the details and that they were coming. And I—didn't know what to tell her."

A long, heavy silence fell, and it wrapped itself around me like ants crawling all over my skin.

He hadn't started yelling, or told me to go fuck myself. That was something?

"My family won't be there," he said at last. "That wasn't part of the deal. And it's not going to happen. Your family wouldn't want them there in the first place. Sorry."

That last word sounded perfunctory, insincere, like he knew he ought to say it but hated the necessity. I didn't blame him for not wanting to apologize for any inconvenience. Because my family *didn't* want them there, they didn't even want Dimitri there, and I had no grounds to contradict him.

Okay. No arguing. But I knew how to negotiate, and that I could do without being an asshole.

"Look," I began tentatively, "I know you haven't talked to me much about your family." At all, really, unless you counted that one anecdote he'd told about his mother making him read Russian classics. And I couldn't bring that up. Letting him know how closely I'd hugged that story to my chest, one of the only crumbs of his real self he'd given me, would make me look as pathetic as I was. "But if there's something I can do to make it happen, we could make it part of the deal. If you need some—support from me."

"Support," he said flatly. "You mean money. More money than the hundred grand you already gave me."

"Do you have any idea what my family's spending on this reception? Believe me, money's not the—"

"I don't want a single fucking penny from your *family*," he snarled, turning in his seat to glare at me, fangs dropping. "I wouldn't take it if I was starving."

"Where the fuck do you think my money came from?" I demanded, blood pressure skyrocketing so fast my arms went numb. I had to clench my hands around the steering wheel for dear life. If he hated my family that much, hated their money that much, and I was a part of that family no matter how much I hated them too…fuck, I couldn't drive like this, the cars in front of me had gone blurry.

I wrenched the steering wheel, pulling us over into the right lane to a chorus of honking and then turning abruptly into the strip mall we were passing by, managing to get us into a parking spot behind a fast-food place. We came to a stop with a jerk as I slammed the brakes too hard.

"I think the money you paid me came from your own hard work," Dimitri practically shouted, and when I turned to face him the rage in his had me flinching away. I'd never seen him like this. "And I hate that it came from your family indirectly, but that is what it is. You want to pay me to get you what you want? Fucking fine. But I'm not letting *them* pay me to trot my family out like performing monkeys to make them look good. Fuck them. Not happening, Brook!"

His hands flexed, claws gleaming where they'd started to pop out of his fingers as he lost control of his shift.

And that scared me even more.

"Fuck," he said heavily, after a moment of tense silence. "Fuck,

Brook, I wouldn't hurt you. You know that. Don't look at me like that. Please."

"Like what?" I dragged my gaze away from those deadly claws and back up to his. The deep, golden glow in his eyes and the fangs he hadn't retracted didn't reassure me much.

He swallowed hard, Adam's apple bobbing. "Like you're afraid of me. Shit. Brook, I fucking hate your parents. And your brother. Maybe that's not what you want to hear. But it's the truth. I'm not doing anything for them. I'd do nearly any—I'll do what you paid me for. But my family stays out of this fucking mess. And believe me, you and your parents wouldn't want them there. Please take my word for it."

If he thought of me as anything remotely like a real mate, he'd want me to meet his family, wouldn't he? He'd want them involved.

But he didn't.

You and your parents. As if we were united in this, and he had to protect his family not only from my parents and brother but from me.

The coldness had spread, now, from my chest into my limbs, seeping poison that left me numb and lethargic. I tried to get a fix on the bond, but I couldn't sense anything but anger and some other negative emotion: resignation, maybe.

Either way, nothing good.

"Can you at least tell me—" I cut myself off. No. I didn't have any right to ask why they couldn't come, why he thought I wouldn't want them to, or if there even was another reason beyond the sufficient one of him simply not wanting them to be exposed to my family's snobbery.

"Okay," I sighed. I rubbed at my aching temples, hoping he couldn't see how shaky my hands had gotten. "I'll think of something to tell my mother. It's okay with you if I make up whatever I think is most likely to get her to drop it, right? Pregnant sister who can't travel, mom staying home to take care of her. Whatever. Something she can't argue with. Will you back me up on whatever story I think of? It won't be anything that makes them look bad."

"They can think of stuff that makes my family look bad all on their own, right? I bet they already have."

I dropped my hand and glanced up sharply. Jesus, how did he know? It must have shown on my face, because he let out a short, bitter little laugh.

"Yeah, you don't need to say anything. I know what they probably think of me, my background. They aren't even necessarily wrong." He sighed, shook his head, and—reached out, taking my hand in his. He'd gotten his claws in, finally, and the way he touched me couldn't have been more gentle. A frown drew his brows together. "Scale of one to ten, Brook. How close are you to having a seizure right now?"

I let out a long, shaky breath. My eyes still wouldn't quite focus.

Well, shit. And he'd noticed before I had.

"Maybe a six," I said, too drained to try to lie. Besides, I couldn't drive like this, and that I couldn't hide. We might be werewolves with a healing ability that'd make a car accident no big deal, but the same wasn't true of everyone else on the road.

"Okay. Fuck. Okay. We're going to switch places, and I'm going to get you home. In bed, resting. Come on." Without waiting for me to answer, he clicked his seat belt and hopped out, opening my door a second later.

I could've gotten myself out of the car and into the passenger seat, and half of me wanted to snap at him that I wasn't an invalid and didn't need to be babied.

But it felt too good to be taken care of for once, rather than shoved out of sight like a shameful secret when my Hensley's symptoms recurred. Dimitri's careful hands guiding me out of the car, his strong arm around my waist, his murmured reassurances that everything would be fine, that I only needed to breathe deeply and relax, hit an exposed nerve that I couldn't muster the energy to protect, not right then.

He got me settled and even leaned into the car, barely fitting his bulk around me, to get my seat belt fastened for me. I tipped my head back, closed my eyes, and took a deep, soothing inhale of the scent of him. Warm, tart, spicy. My mate, filling all of my senses.

The shakiness subsided slightly, and my heart started to slow.

"That's good, Brook," he said softly. "Good." His hand brushed over the side of my face, thumb stroking my cheek so quickly I almost thought I'd imagined it. "We'll be home in no time."

The door shut, and he got in the other side and started the car. Home. Not just my house, but *home*…because it had Dimitri living in it with me.

Chapter 15
Ready and Waiting

I woke up when the sun had already gone most of the way down—late, in other words, because tomorrow would be the summer solstice, and the sun didn't set until nine-thirty or so. Dimitri had half-carried me into the house and tucked me into bed, stripping me down to my boxers gently but efficiently.

If I'd had any doubts about his level of attraction to me, that would've settled them. He didn't linger and he didn't ogle. There were no unnecessary touches.

Luckily, I was too out of it to get hard from him undressing me—and I had to admit I probably would have under other circumstances, no matter how perfunctory he was about it.

Sitting up in bed didn't take much effort, my muscles responding without any unpleasant surprises and my vision staying as clear as it ever did. When I fumbled my glasses off the nightstand and put them on, I could see just fine.

Apparently the potential seizure had been headed off at the pass.

I almost wished it hadn't, because then I might've had an excuse for avoiding the rest of the conversation we'd been having in the car.

Dimitri stuck his head through my half-open bedroom door by the time I'd swung my legs over the side of the bed. "Should you be getting up? I'll help you."

He stepped into the room, but I waved him off.

"I'm fine, seriously." I got up under my own power and headed for the bathroom. No more heartwrenchingly sweet and tender care from my very fake and very temporary mate, or I might have a seizure after all. "I'll see you downstairs, just going to grab a shower," I threw over my shoulder, and I shut the bathroom door without waiting for an answer.

Oh, fuck. It hit me as I reached for the shower knob, and I hustled back to open the door again. "Dimitri?"

He was still standing there in my bedroom, staring at the bathroom door with a weird expression on his face. Dammit, did he really think I'd fall down and hit my head or something? I was fine!

"Yeah, Brook? You need something?"

I shook my head. "I'm sorry. I forgot to thank you. For driving me home and getting me in bed. So—thank you. That was really nice of you."

The words sounded as stilted as they felt coming out of my mouth, and my cheeks burned with embarrassment.

But Dimitri's lips quirked in that half-smile of his, and his eyes warmed. "You're welcome," he said, in that low, almost-growl that never failed to make a shiver run down my spine. This time it didn't stop there, the vibration of his voice landing somewhere south of my tailbone. "I'll make dinner."

He left my bedroom before I could do something incredibly stupid, like beg him to get in the shower with me.

I didn't dare jerk off, knowing he'd be able to scent it on me. But when my hands started to wander, the water beating down to cover any sounds I might make, I didn't force myself to stop, allowing myself a moment of indulgence. Two fingers crammed into my hole, slick with soap, were nothing more than a horrible tease: not big enough, not hot enough…not *him*.

I yanked them out, miserable and aching and unsatisfied, and started to wash up.

Dinner. Finishing our talk. Not that there was a whole lot more to say, though. I only had to make sure I had his buy-in on telling my mother a passel of lies, and then—

With a high-pitched yelp, I jumped and flailed and barely caught myself before I slipped as the bathroom door opened suddenly with enough force to bounce off the wall.

I watched wide-eyed and frozen in shock as Dimitri stalked into the bathroom, glowing golden-gray eyes fixed on me as he started to tear off his clothes. He'd changed out of his suit at some point while I slept, and his T-shirt and jeans were on the floor in five seconds flat.

And then he opened the shower door and stepped in with me, crowding me against the wall.

"What," I stammered. "What?"

Without a word, still staring down at me with an intense, unreadable expression in those eyes, he trailed his hand down over my stomach, my muscles clenching as he touched me, brushed his fingers over my erection, and slipped them between my legs. They found their target unerringly, two fingertips slipping into my hole without resistance.

I gasped, trying to spread my legs as much as I could without losing my balance. His hand still felt enormous shoved between my thighs. Awkward. Like it shouldn't fit there.

Perfect.

"I knew you were getting yourself off. I knew, and I had to— you were already doing this," he growled, and shifted closer, hemming me in against the wall. My back hit the tiles. And Dimitri's other hand flew up, pressing across my throat and pinning me there. "You were fingering your pretty hole, Brook. Don't try to tell me different."

I might've answered, but he shoved his fingers in so deep I moaned instead, squeezing my eyes shut. "Look at me while I fuck you open," he commanded me, all alpha, and I opened them again, unable to break his gaze as he twisted his fingers and screwed them into me almost brutally hard.

His eyes filled my vision completely, and I wanted to close my own so badly, to break that connection, to keep him from seeing right through me and into my mental turmoil, like looking through a sheet of fractured glass.

But he'd told me what to do, and I couldn't help it.

Dimitri finger-fucked me ruthlessly, thrusting his hand deeper until I went up on my toes, the hand on my throat shifting to keep me up as I did, dangling helplessly between his grip on my neck and his fist between my legs. My whole body juddered against the tiles. If he hadn't been pinning me by the neck, my head would've slammed into the wall, but I couldn't move anything but my arms—and I grabbed onto his shoulders, clinging on for dear life.

The three fingers pulled out partway, and he adjusted his hand.

Oh, no.

"Dimitri, I can't," I choked out. "I can't take—"

"Yes, you fucking can," he snarled, and forced four fingers into my body, eyes never leaving mine, his pupils dilated to black pools behind the gold.

I couldn't, I couldn't, and he was going to rip me in half—except that I came like that, hips jerking helplessly into the empty air, my body seizing up around his hand and clenching almost painfully.

Slumped against the tiles, so cold against my back with the heat of the shower and his body at my front, I felt like reality had slipped away: clouds of steam, the harsh panting of our breaths, my throat tight beneath his palm. And most of his hand still half-buried inside my well-used ass, not moving now, but *there*. Like he owned me and could just…leave it there, if he wanted.

It felt surreal. And I still couldn't move or look away from him, caught as much by his focused attention as by his hands on me and in me.

The hand on my throat slid up, cupping my chin. Dimitri's gaze dropped to my lips. He ran his thumb over the lower one, tugging it down, pushing his thumb between my teeth to open my mouth. And then again, rubbing over my lips, rough but not careless, deliberate in the way he showed me he could touch me any way he wanted. His thumb dipped inside again and pressed down on my tongue. Slowly, agonizingly slowly, he withdrew his fingers from my hole, letting me down off my tiptoes.

As my heels touched the ground, he took half a step back.

Waiting.

I managed to tear my gaze from his at last, my eyes tracing the rivulets of water running down the column of his throat, between his pecs, along the trail of dark hair over his abdomen.

His cock stood up almost straight between us, glistening with water and with a few pearly-white traces of my come.

I shuddered, transfixed by the sight.

Dimitri let his thumb slip out of my mouth and slid his hand up again, until he had his fingers clenched in my hair.

I slid down the wall, his hand moving with me, guiding me, until I folded to my knees in front of him, his cock inches from my face.

Leaning in close enough to kiss it took the smallest motion. My lips brushed over his thick, swollen cockhead, our mingled scents rising up and making my head spin. I flicked out my tongue and tasted myself on his velvety skin.

I chased those traces of my own come, sliding my lips down his shaft, licking it up. Teasing, tasting, scenting him, eyes drooping half-shut as I fell into a fugue, lulled by the drumming of the shower, grounded by the hand in my hair keeping my head steady.

It seemed like he let me go on like that forever, up one side of his cock and down the other, pausing in between to lap at the head or nuzzle his heavy balls.

But finally his patience ran out, and he tugged on my hair, tipping my head back.

My mouth opened obediently to that silent command, and he pushed his cock in, thrusting shallowly, gently, not trying to go too deep. It wasn't anything like the first time I'd sucked his cock. He didn't demand anything, didn't even seem like he was trying to get off. Dimitri didn't need to demand anything, because I was his for the taking. Passive, ready and waiting for whatever he chose to do to me. He could use me slowly if that's what he wanted, tease himself with my lips and tongue. Or he could fuck my throat, choke me on his cock, and I'd still take it.

But he wanted this, and so I held my mouth open and savored every motion of his thick erection, filling my mouth and withdrawing, hot and slick.

With a low, incoherent sound, Dimitri pulled back, letting his cock rest on my lower lip, and wrapped his other hand around the shaft.

He started to stroke it, a steady rhythm clearly designed to bring himself off, only the head pushing in and out of my mouth.

At last his hand sped up, and his stomach muscles clenched, abs going rigid.

The first spurt filled my mouth, trickling down into my throat, but I couldn't swallow, not yet, because he hadn't pulled out of me. More spilled out of the corners of my mouth, slicking my chin and throat. Another spasm, and Dimitri let out a bitten-off groan, pulling his cock back so that he painted my cheeks and mouth, the bitter, salty scent and flavor of him overwhelming my senses.

He rubbed his cockhead over my lips, back and forth, across my cheek, back into my mouth for a moment to coat my tongue with his come. I dared to look up at him through my lashes, and his face tightened, a muscle jumping in his jaw. Those eyes hadn't lost any of their intensity, fixed on my face all covered in his come, my body still folded up on my knees at his feet with his hand holding my head in place, throat bared.

We stayed there for an endless moment, gazing into each other's eyes. I didn't know what he saw in mine. Whatever it was, I couldn't hide it—so it didn't really matter.

Not much seemed to matter, right then.

And his expression was completely inscrutable. I had no idea what he was thinking.

That didn't matter much either. I'd submitted to my mate, my alpha. Whatever he was thinking, he had to be satisfied with me. And that was enough.

At last he let me go, slowly and carefully so that my head didn't fall back against the shower wall. It drooped down, all my muscles going limp at once. Dimitri crouched down and got his arms around me, lifting me up, cradling me against his chest.

When he shifted me so that my head leaned on his shoulder, I left my eyes closed, not moving as he washed my face and rinsed between my legs. My hole felt so open and stretched, swollen and almost sore. It'd heal within half an hour or so. I knew I'd miss the sensation when it did.

At least I could still taste him when I licked my puffy lips.

"Jesus fuck, Brook," Dimitri muttered.

I opened my eyes a crack in time to see him staring at my mouth, eyes all wide and dark.

"Mmm," I managed.

"Fuck." He shook his head like he wanted to clear it, hair spattering water across my face. "Fuck, sorry. God. Do you want dinner?"

Dinner. Yeah, I really, really did, and at the thought my stomach let out a ferociously loud growl.

"I'll take that as a yes." Dimitri bundled me against his chest again and shut the shower off. "As soon as I get you resting, I'll go cook. I should've cooked already. I don't know what I was..." He trailed off, not bothering to finish.

After he'd given us both a quick rub-down with a towel, he half-carried, half-dragged me into my bedroom, deposited me on the bed, tossed the sheet over me, and went out the door, presumably to make dinner.

Lying there in the quiet, replaying everything in my head...well, for one thing, my cock started filling again, and that annoyed me, because Dimitri was downstairs and unable to do anything about it. But for another—that had been so out of character for me. Hadn't it? All those thoughts about Dimitri being my alpha. About doing what he wanted me to do.

Had the mate bond changed me so much?

Had I changed? Or had I been forcing a role on myself all these years, trying to stay in control in one small (very small, sadly, because I never had time for dating) area of my life?

It didn't matter much, I thought woozily, rolling over onto my back with a sigh. Jesus, that felt good. Lying back. Not caring. All naked and clean and well-fucked, with my mate cooking me dinner downstairs.

It'd all work itself out.

Somewhere in the back of my mind, I knew it damn well wouldn't.

But right then, I didn't care. And it was bliss.

Chapter 16

Your Father Smells Funny

My mother called me the next morning when Dimitri and I were halfway to the office. One benefit of that horrifically embarrassing visit of theirs the day we'd mated was that she'd stopped showing up on my doorstep.

On the other hand…

"Brook!" she screeched, the speakerphone failing to contain her evident irritation. "I have been waiting for you to get back to me on the issue of…Dimitri's…family, even though I doubt—"

Oh, shit. "He's in the car with me!" I practically shouted, desperate to interrupt her before she could share whatever rude, insulting thing was about to come out of her mouth.

As she fell silent, seething palpably even across several miles and a couple of cell towers, I glanced over at Dimitri in the passenger seat. His half-lidded eyes, loose necktie, and unbuttoned top shirt button gave the accurate impression of a man who hadn't been happy about getting up at six. Well, too bad for him. I had a seven-thirty breakfast meeting.

He shrugged and closed his eyes.

Thanks a fucking bundle.

"Brook, are you listening?"

She hadn't been talking, dammit!

"I'm right here. And I spoke to Dimitri about his family last night. Unfortunately, his sister's been put on bed rest for a high-risk pregnancy and his mother's unable to leave her until she's given birth. Or for a while after," I added hastily, hedging my bets. The party was coming up—shit, within the next couple of weeks. But I wouldn't put it past my mother to reschedule it, no matter how much she hated that kind of thing, simply to paint me into a corner. She could be petty like that.

"They won't be able to make it," I continued. "I'm sure you'll be able to find a way to make all the guests understand the circumstances." The building silence on her end had an ominous, the-tornado's-heading-your-way quality to it. Fuck, fuck, duck and cover... "They'll be more focused on you as the hostess, anyway," I went on desperately. "Everyone wants an invitation to one of your parties. They're legendary."

And they were, if you happened to be a middle-aged Idahoan social climber. But details. Flattery could get you everywhere, right?

It could at least get you partially out of trouble, as it turned out. "Fine," she said tightly. "I suppose there's nothing you can do about it if they're too gauche to understand their social obligations. You have communicated our position as one of the most prominent packs in the west, haven't you?"

Halfway through letting out a long breath of relief, I nearly choked. In other words, didn't they know how far we were condescending by forming a mating alliance with them? And Dimitri was listening to this! But another glance to the side showed me the same picture of sleepy indifference. If she'd offended him, I couldn't tell. Maybe he'd reached peak offense and simply no longer cared.

"I'm sure they regret not being able to attend even more than they would have otherwise," I managed, sounding a lot dryer than I'd have liked.

Thank fuck, she let it pass with only a sniff of disdain.

"Then we'll need to rearrange the receiving line. All right. Any more surprises for me, Brook, or may I assume that the reception will otherwise go off without a hitch?"

Blake would almost certainly find some way to ruin it for everyone, whether by causing a drunken scene or trying to publicly humiliate me, or both, but no point in mentioning that.

"No. No more surprises." If I banged my forehead into the steering wheel, I might hit the SUV in front of me, and then I'd miss my breakfast meeting. Dammit. "We'll be ready for our part of it, and of course you can tell me if I can help with any of the final arrangements." Shit, I really didn't remember when it was supposed to be. No way I could admit that. "Have you sent details to Jackie yet, or do I need to fill her in?"

"She's fully informed. You can ask her to remind you, since you clearly have no idea what's going on." I winced. She might not like me much, but she did know me, apparently. "Brook, you're very lucky that your family understands what's necessary to maintain our position in…" And she was off to the races.

She kept it up full-steam until, with a silent prayer of gratitude, I pulled into my spot in the Castelli Industries parking lot. "I have to go, I'm at the office," I interrupted her, and she hung up after a couple more sharp words about my inattention.

The company. The only excuse my mother ever deemed acceptable for blowing her off.

No wonder I was such a workaholic.

I shut down the engine and turned to Dimitri. He'd gotten his shirt and tie arranged sometime during my mother's monologue, and he sat there looking at me grimly, outwardly ready for a day at the office. And inwardly? Christ, how the fuck would I know? We'd barely spoken the night before or this morning, eating dinner together quietly, going to bed separately, and getting up and getting ready without more than the necessary exchange of a few sentences about who'd made the coffee.

It was like the Dimitri who'd taken me apart in the shower and the Dimitri sitting beside me were two separate men, and they liked to pretend not to know each other.

And no matter how much I'd come to unwillingly depend on one of them, and crave the other, I didn't understand either of them particularly well, either.

"You were listening to all of that?"

He nodded. "I'll go where I'm told and behave myself, like always," he said without any enthusiasm.

The early hour, my mother's sparkling personality having its inevitable effect, or some other source of reluctance?

Prying into his private business yet again, when he'd made it so clear he didn't see it as *my* business, might backfire so badly. The dashboard clock read 7:12. Barely enough time to prep for that meeting. I was never late to meetings, never anything but five minutes early and completely up to speed on the topics to be addressed.

But…maybe this was more important.

For once, I had to take a moment to be me. Not a VP of Castelli Industries, not a more-or-less-willing participant in my family's obsession with the company and the pack's status.

Just a man, with a mate who clearly had something weighing on his mind.

I couldn't think of a way to ease into it, though. Not with the clock ticking, and not after that horror-show of a call with my mother.

"Will you tell me why they really can't come?" I asked abruptly. Dimitri's face closed off completely, eyes flashing, and I quickly added, "Please? And not because I want to put pressure on you. Not because my mother's being a bitch about it. We were talking about it yesterday, and then I got sick and we had to drop it. But I don't even know if you were okay with the excuse I gave. I understand you don't want them to have anything to do with my family, believe me," I went on, desperate for him to give me something. Anything. To show me that he trusted me, even just a little bit. "You said they wouldn't want them there anyway. But I'm not my family. And I— I'm not them."

The anger faded from his expression as I talked, replaced with something closer to—shame? It looked like shame, and felt like it, too, from what I could pick up through the bond.

He stared out the windshield at the blinding sunlight reflecting off of the building's expanses of blue-tinted glass. If I did that, I wouldn't be able to see for hours. Stupid alphas.

The clock changed to 7:13. I forced myself not to fidget.

Finally he said, quickly and very low, and still not meeting my eyes, "My mother's in a wheelchair. Broken back a long time ago. She's human."

I stared at him in shock, everything I'd assumed about the money I'd paid him flying straight out the window. He'd said it was personal. A family issue. And like a prick, I'd thought—as much as I'd thought about it at all—that he meant something like an equally deadbeat brother with gambling debts or something. Not this.

And Dimitri had hidden this from me. Because he didn't trust me? Maybe, but...a cold, sick ache had taken hold of the pit of my stomach, fed by the way he'd insisted that we wouldn't want his family at the reception to begin with. He knew how my family operated: alphas at the top of the pile, and then werewolves, and then—distantly—other shifters, and finally humans. An imperfect werewolf, like me, wasn't worth much.

Let alone a human woman with a serious medical condition.

Did he truly, honestly, think I'd agree? That I'd be disgusted? Or…embarrassed to be mated into a family like that? My mother certainly would be. She'd be horrified beyond belief.

Imagining her reaction and the pain it would cause Dimitri and his mother made me want to sink through the floor of the car and the asphalt beneath, covering my face and groaning the whole way down.

Dimitri had to be brought to understand that I didn't feel like that. He *had* to, and the desire to explain myself, even though he hadn't directly accused me, built almost into panic. I opened and closed my mouth, unable to find any words that wouldn't sound patronizing or defensive or like pointless platitudes.

But I'd waited too long to answer, and Dimitri reached for the door handle, saying roughly, "It's not your problem. We should go insi—"

"No, wait!" I grabbed his arm, the muscles rigid with straining tension beneath my fingers. "Wait," I said again, my voice shaking. He stopped moving, but he didn't let go of the door. I only had one shot at this, I knew that instinctively. He wouldn't bring it up again, and he wouldn't let me talk about it, either. "You're right that it's not my problem, because it's not a problem for me. Shit, I don't mean that it's not a problem—of course it's a problem. Not that your mother's a problem! Fuck, I'm sorry, I—please forget all of that and let me start over!"

Dimitri turned back to me slowly, his hand relaxing on the door handle and the bicep beneath my fingers unbunching a bit. The sad twist to his lips made my heart ache, but when he looked at me, I didn't see anything but understanding in his eyes.

"You know, a lot of problems could be solved by people just giving each other the benefit of the doubt," he said quietly. "That was about as clear as mud, Brook." My cheeks heated, and I bit my lip, and—my breath caught as he reached up and smoothed his thumb over my mouth, releasing that bit of flesh from my teeth. His hand dropped before I could do something incredibly stupid, like kiss it. "But I think I understand what you mean anyway. You don't think having a human mother's some kind of stain on my character, right? And you don't look down on someone for not being strong. Physically, I mean. She's the strongest person I know in other ways."

I shook my head vehemently, afraid my voice would crack if I tried to speak.

What an asshole I'd been, pitying myself for my Hensley's—which amounted to little more than an inconvenience, honestly, or would if my family didn't treat it like a deep, deadly secret. And turning up my nose at Dimitri's need for money. To be fair, he'd owed sixty grand. But how much of that had been borrowed to pay for his mother's care in the first place?

I'd be willing to bet every penny of it.

Dimitri smiled, still a little forced, a little tense. But a smile all the same. "I have a sister, too," he added. "She's not pregnant, though. And your excuse works just fine. Thanks. For covering for me."

"You're welcome," I whispered. "But you don't owe me any thanks. Thank you for telling me. I wish I could me—" I cut myself off, pretending to cough. Meet them? Dimitri would only want that if our mating was real. And I had no right to ask, no matter how much the thought of being treated as if it was made me yearn.

Stupid. I was so stupid.

"You're going to be late for your meeting," Dimitri said. "We should go in."

But he didn't say it in a way that meant he regretted telling me about his mom, and that was enough for me.

I got to my meeting two minutes late in the end.

But I couldn't bring myself to regret that, either.

The way Dimitri had owned me the night before hadn't felt nearly as intimate as those few words, that sign of trust, that he'd given me this morning. And it warmed me from the inside out.

***

"Brook, I need a minute alone with you," Dimitri whispered directly into my ear, clearly wanting to dodge the acute hearing of the alpha weres filing out of the large conference room all around us. I shot everyone a smile, leaning into him as if he'd been saying something sweet to his mate, and I let him tow me around the corner and into a cramped filing room, even though I was inwardly seething with impatience.

After my breakfast meeting, I'd had an hour of calls, punctuated by Jackie popping in to tell me that my mother had scheduled the reception not for two weeks from now, but for this coming Saturday. That had nearly given me a heart attack, and only partially because I hadn't even gotten Dimitri a tuxedo yet.

Dimitri in a tux. There was a mental image I simultaneously wished I could frame and glue to the wall in my brain, and erase before it made me crazy.

Then the second my last call ended, Dimitri and I both went straight to an executive strategy session headed by my father. That had taken three endless, agonizing hours, and we'd just broken for lunch. Even with Dimitri running interference, I'd been the target of most of my father's snide remarks.

That I'd grown used to over the years, but…fuck, I had *so much* actual work to do. Three clients were waiting for progress reports, and I only had good news for one of them. First hours spent being subtly and not-so-subtly ripped up in front of an audience, and now an additional delay.

When Dimitri shut the door behind us, my blood felt like it had heated to boiling in my veins, my mind a tangled, fuzzy mess of competing priorities all demanding attention at once.

"What?" I snapped. "Seriously, what can't wait for later? I don't have time to eat as it is, and I need coffee, at least!"

"I'll get you some coffee and something to eat in a minute. Brook, focus for a second, fuck!" With an effort I felt down to my bones, I lowered my phone, which had buzzed with incoming email notifications the instant I took it off silent. "This is important."

Had he brought me in here to shove me up against one of those filing cabinets and fuck me? Because that might be worth sacrificing lunch, and even coffee—if I had to.

"Look, there's no way to phrase this that won't sound weird," Dimitri said once I'd given him my full, albeit impatient, attention. "But have you noticed that your father smells funny?"

I gaped at him. "Smells...funny? *Funny*?" He'd dragged me in here to tell me my father smelled...*funny*? What next, was he going to tell me my mother was a hamster? "Are you out of your fucking mind?"

Dimitri rolled his eyes and crossed his arms, moving over a foot to block the door. Dammit. He'd anticipated my next move, which was dashing around him and escaping.

"No, I'm not, and don't get all hung up on the word. Weird. Strange. Unusual. I'm not fucking Roget, okay? He smells wrong. And his scent changes from one time I see him to another."

"That's—what are you even on about?" I sputtered, rubbing a hand over my face. Jesus. I did not have time for this. "No one else has ever said anything. And he always smells the same to me. I mean, not like I'm spending a lot of time scenting my father!"

"I don't know what anyone else picks up, because I'm not them. But I've always had a sensitive nose, even for a shifter. It's kind of a mixed blessing. High school sucked." He pulled a face at me, and I couldn't help a half-hearted chuckle. That really would've been the worst. As I watched in fascination, a faint red flush spread over his cheekbones. "I could scent you touching yourself from downstairs in the kitchen," he mumbled, his eyes focusing somewhere over my left shoulder instead of on mine. "Last night."

A ragged, searing bolt of pure want zinged down my spine, a dull, needy ache starting somewhere south. Last night. Four of his fingers stuffing my ass, his cockhead on my tongue, the shower floor bruising my kneecaps...no, fuck, I couldn't. I had to concentrate on the here and now.

His gaze flicked back to me, dropping to my lips, and his chest rose and fell visibly. The air between us thickened like honey.

The here and now wasn't helping with the concentration issue all that much.

"My father," I rasped. "We were talking about—my father." Nothing less sexy than that. I forced myself to give Dimitri's bizarre opinion of my father's scent some honest consideration. If nothing else, I wouldn't get out of here until I did. Dimitri was too stubborn. "Okay, so he smells different sometimes. And I—I guess I'm always more focused on what his scent's telling me about his mood, not the, like, the baseline." Shifter scents had a lot of layers to them; when you paid attention to one set of cues, and got used to discarding the others, you could miss things. That was true enough. "But he might be doing some kind of treatment for his Hensley's symptoms, blood thinners or something," I whispered, even though I knew no one was lurking in the hall. We would've heard them or smelled them there. "That would change things, right? You'd notice that?"

"Yeah, I would," he said slowly, as if giving my words the same amount of thought. "I guess it could be that, except it doesn't smell medicinal. It's something…I'm having trouble defining it. Like the way magic smells. And something like the way an alpha smells. Like the way alpha magic feels, only in a scent," he finished, sounding as frustrated as I felt by his inability to put it into adequate words. "Either way. I've noticed he's more of an asshole when his scent changes like that. This morning, for example."

Yeah, what the fuck else was new? "Asshole" had been my father's default setting my entire life. I'd tried to take this seriously, I really had, but my phone kept buzzing in my pocket, each vibration puncturing the very last of my remaining patience.

"Dimitri, I really don't have time for this, okay? I'm sorry. Yes. He's an asshole. I'm sorry he 'smells funny' to you, and the alpha magic thing is probably just that his pheromones spike when he's in a pissed-off mood. I need to head to my office now. We have to be back in that meeting in an hour."

Dimitri sighed, glared, and finally shrugged. "Fine. I'll go get you some coffee and a bite to eat downstairs."

Would he really drop the subject so easily? It roused my suspicions, but when he stepped to the side and opened the door for me, it vanished from my mind in the time it took to get out of the filing room and start striding toward my office. Three clients. One hour. Too little time to get things done, and with my father's sneers still ringing in my ears…

Dimitri's distaste for my family had made him paranoid, I figured. And not that I blamed him. Not in the slightest.

But whatever bee he had in his bonnet, I simply didn't have the energy to participate in the insanity.

Chapter 17

Something Brewing

Dimitri in a tux turned out to be ten times more devastating than I'd expected.

"What?" he demanded, sounding cranky as hell, tugging at his bow tie—which I'd just gotten perfect, dammit! "Why are you staring at me? Do I look that stupid?"

"Stop that!" I lunged, trying to yank his hand away, and he dodged me.

"This thing is fucking choking me."

"No, it fucking isn't. Quit acting like a toddler."

Dimitri glared at me so ferociously I might've quailed if I hadn't had his tongue in my ass and his big, claw-tipped hands cradling my hips with impossible gentleness a few hours before.

I had to turn away and pretend to need to brush dust off my shoes to hide my blush. Or try to, anyway. He could probably smell it on me, the bastard.

Of course, I hadn't smelled like much besides the adrenaline-tinged irritation of a workaholic with too much on his plate and the arousal of a man with an extremely attentive mate for the past week.

We hadn't talked about it. In fact, the night after that bizarre conversation about how my father smelled, he'd come to my room after I'd already gone to bed with the lights out—and when I'd tried to ask what he was doing, he'd put his hand over my mouth, yanked the blankets off of me, and proceeded to fuck me through the mattress without a single word of his own.

I'd gotten the message.

And when he repeated the performance the next night, I'd bitten back anything I longed to say or to ask, whimpering quietly into the darkness in lieu of any other communication. The bulk of his muscles and his hot, overwhelming presence made those nighttime visits dreamlike, as in one of those torrid novels with possessive demon lovers coming only when their (mostly willing, let's be real here) victims had fallen into a restive sleep.

Not that I'd ever avidly, secretly read anything like that in college or anything.

Anyway, Dimitri fucked me every night, and once his knot had gone down, he left without speaking. And he didn't acknowledge it in the morning. A couple of times, like last night, he'd eaten me out with hungry, breathtaking force, drawing sounds out of me I hadn't known a human-adjacent being could produce.

And *then* he'd fucked and knotted me. By then, I'd been sobbing with frustration, because every time I tried to beg he put his hand over my mouth again.

We didn't discuss it in the morning, or during the days we spent at the office or ducking out to visit various upscale men's clothiers. Or in the evenings, either, because he'd borrowed a laptop from me and had taken to closing himself up in his bedroom after dinner. Sometimes I heard him on the phone, but he was always speaking Russian.

My one attempt at delicately inquiring had been met with a stonewalling I'd never seen equaled even by a client with a past-due invoice.

Now Saturday had come, and we were due at the club in half an hour, with the guests arriving an hour after that. And we still weren't talking about it. Hundreds of people were about to descend on us, all congratulating us (more or less sincerely) on our mating, and I couldn't even get my own head on straight regarding what our mating really meant.

What it meant to me had changed. That I couldn't deny any more. Every time Dimitri touched me, my skin fizzed with awareness; my whole body lit up like a giant firecracker. His smiles drew answering smiles out of me, welling up helplessly from some place inside me that I hadn't realized could be such a reservoir of effortless happiness until he came along. Even trading grouchy semi-insults with him cheered me up, because the bastard could piss me off and make me laugh simultaneously.

But to him, this was all an unpleasant charade. Even if he came to me every night and fucked me. What he'd said to me when I tried to convince him my pleasure had been a fluke kept running through my mind in an increasingly painful spiral: *Yeah, it got me off. A tight hole will do that. Fucking you is kind of adjacent to what I usually enjoy.*

"Brook? You ready? You okay? Those shoes are pretty fucking shiny already. And this party is exactly the kind of shit that gives you seizures." I jumped and looked up from my very, very shiny shoes, the tissue I'd been using to dust them clenched in my fist. God, he probably thought seizures were the least of my issues.

"I'm fine. Yeah. There was a, a spot on the toe."

He frowned down at me, shrugged, and said, "Well, then let's go. If we're late we're going to hear about it."

I shuddered. If we were late, we might as well be dead, because no other excuse would be sufficient. And my mother would find us beyond the grave to make our lives hell, anyway.

The club wasn't far away, just a couple of miles around the edge of town, nestled between some manicured hills. A golf course, a restaurant and bar, tennis courts and a pool. All the amenities, dressed up in lots of stonework façade and huge shiny glass windows, with antique-looking clocks and lamps and bullshit like that to add what they probably hoped was old-world ambiance. My parents loved this fucking place.

When I handed the keys off to the valet, I had to bite my tongue not to beg him to hide me in the trunk and stash me somewhere I wouldn't be found until tomorrow.

And then Dimitri and I looked at each other, nodded grimly, and went in shoulder to shoulder.

Despite my mother's general disapproval of everything that had led us to this point, the first part of the reception went perfectly smoothly, orchestrated to the nth degree. And no one would ever have known how much she deplored the necessity of it, by her precisely calculated smiles and sophisticated small-talk. Lanterns hung from every tree, waiters circulated with probably delicious hors d'oeuvres that I didn't have a chance to get any of, champagne flowed, and bubbles of chatter and laughter rose up, mingling with the splash of a couple of fountains and the soft strains of party-appropriate music.

Probably awesome if you were there as a guest, but Dimitri and I were trapped near the entrance with my parents and Blake, greeting everyone as they arrived, and, in my case at least, starting to go lightheaded with boredom, my cheeks aching from the force of my polite smiles.

And after a while, it became more than that. I could feel something brewing, a heaviness in the atmosphere. It hadn't quite reached the level of something wicked this way coming, but close. My father had mustered an appropriate level of courtesy for the guests, but every time one of them wasn't observing him, his brows drew together, his face setting into lines of—I didn't know what. Pain? Annoyance? He didn't seem altogether well, either way.

Blake's usual smarmy self-satisfaction had a brittle, edgy quality to it, expressed in his laughter at the guests' jokes being a bit too loud and a bit too sharp, and in the venomous glances he shot my way now and then.

And Dimitri was like a statue by my side, solid and dependable, but so tense he could've broken bricks with his jaw. He kept subtly sniffing the air. Scenting my father? I thought he might be scenting my father. Christ, he was *nuts*. Everyone around me had gone fucking crazy. Maybe they were all pod people and I was Donald Sutherland.

The flow of arriving guests had slowed to a trickle. In a sizable gap between groups, I turned to Dimitri, whispering out of the corner of my mouth, "Do you feel it too? Something's up, right? And stop sniffing, you psycho!"

"I feel it," he muttered back, leaning down by my ear and slipping an arm around my waist, like we were having a private mate moment. Even though I knew why he was touching me, and that it wasn't because he simply wanted to, it still made me quiver. "But you didn't want to hear it the other day, Brook. You ready to listen now?"

Ready to listen…? What the fuck could my father's odd scent have to do with the strained, unnatural behavior of everyone around me?

"Cut the PDA, Creek," Blake snapped from behind me. "Act your age."

"Brook!" my mother gasped. "Don't upset your brother! You know he's sensitive."

I spun on them both, startled and goaded past endurance. "Sensitive? He's as sensitive as a—"

"Don't you dare finish that sentence," my father interjected heavily, face flushing an ugly, dusky red. God, could Dimitri be on to something? Because he didn't sound good, either. "This isn't the time for your petty envy and rivalry."

"*My* petty—*envy*? Are you—I don't envy Blake!" As the words left my mouth, I wished desperately that I could call them back. In their minds, of course I envied Blake, the tall, handsome alpha brother with no Hensley's and no disgusting eyeglasses displaying my imperfection to the world. And even those few words of rebellion against the family's creed that being an alpha werewolf was the universe's most desirable possible state would be enough to set my father off like a match to a pool of gasoline.

I could see it starting in the swelling of his chest, the clenching of his fists, that vein in his temple going wild.

But Blake got there first.

"You'll envy me when I'm your boss," he snarled, lips twisted and eyes glinting with malice. "You keep clinging to this delusion that if you try hard enough, you'll be the CEO someday. Wait until you're doing what I tell you, you little asshole!"

That hit me like a punch to the gut, and the world went bright and hazy around me, everything lit up like highbeams in fog.

"What?" My voice didn't sound, or feel, like it belonged to me. It came from far, far away, hoarse and echoing. "What did you say?"

My parents were both arguing, with each other or with Blake, and he'd started expostulating with them, but it buzzed in my ears like static.

Dimitri's voice cut through it, clear and real. "We should go discuss this somewhere private."

"You have no place in this, you lowlife upstart—"

And Dimitri interrupted my father without hesitation, possibly the only person to have ever done so in my presence. "You'll do what I say, or I'll take the microphone over there and tell all these rich, snotty friends of yours that you're not really an alpha."

***

The quiet private meeting room the club management had found for us in a big fucking hurry could've held at least thirty people, but just the six of us made it feel horrifically claustrophobic.

Six, because Dimitri had insisted—his voice still low enough to keep anyone else from hearing, and his tone even and measured— that our pack shaman be brought along.

We faced off in a circle of sorts, my mother seated stiffly in an armchair near the fireplace, eyes glittering with fury, hands clenched in her silk-clad lap. Blake hovered at her shoulder, red-faced with fury after my father had told him to shut up when he started whining.

And my father and Prescott, our shaman, stood a few feet away, reeking of anger...and of fear.

Fear. Because Dimitri, who stood calmly beside me, had terrified them both.

None of it made any sense. It had to be pure nonsense. Didn't it? Not an alpha? Where the hell had he gotten that from? I couldn't focus, couldn't grasp a single thought long enough to analyze it, all of it slipping away faster and faster the harder I tried to grab on.

Blake. CEO. All my work for nothing.

Mating Dimitri, for nothing. If I'd never met him, I'd never have been able to lose him. And if my plan had been doomed from the beginning, he had no reason to stay past tonight.

I was about to lose everything.

My head felt like it was on a string, bobbing wildly somewhere over my body, and my limbs hung numb and heavy.

The door shut as the manager who'd escorted us here fled with a minimum of grace, more flustered than I'd thought someone in customer service could get.

My father fixed Dimitri with a hard stare filled with hatred. "You will retract this absurd allegation. You will do precisely as you're told, or I'll ruin you and anyone associated with you. And when I announce my upcoming retirement and Blake's instatement as CEO, you'll both be his most dedicated supporters."

"Why now?" I demanded, a lifetime of obedience, of not rocking the boat, finally losing its grip on me as panic and despair took over. Blake? As CEO? I'd always been so certain it was impossible, that my father knew that as well as I did. "Why retire now, and Blake? He doesn't know the first thing about—"

"You and this unsuitable alpha of yours will bolster his position while he finds his footing!" my father shouted. "That was always the plan, the reason why I'd decided to choose an alpha mate for you." That hit me like a thunderbolt. He'd never meant to promote me. Never…God. Sweat broke out on my forehead, and my fists clenched involuntarily. "Your failure to understand your place in this family has disappointed me, and your mother, your entire life, but you'll understand it now and do your duty to me and to your brother. Or I'll cut you off. I'll break your grandfather's trust, Brook. I'll make it impossible for you and—this," and he gestured at Dimitri, "to amount to more than what you would have without us. Which is to say, nothing."

"No, you won't," Dimitri said grimly. "Enough bluffing."

"Bluffing? You worthless—"

"Enough!" Dimitri didn't raise his voice more than a little, but it cut through my father's bluster like a knife through jelly, and everyone in the room startled, staring. "Enough bullshit," he said, low and deadly. "Everyone in this room knows you have Hensley's Syndrome."

Blake let out a sharp, high crack of laughter. "Hensley's? Are you out of your mind? Brook has Hensley's. Dad can't have it, he's an alpha! It's—it's impossible," he faltered.

Dimitri bared his teeth at Blake, his alpha magic spiking, a tangible presence in the room. A soft whimper left my lips. Blake went white and fell back a step, gripping onto the side of our mother's chair.

"Okay, I was wrong," Dimitri growled. "Almost everyone in this room knew you had Hensley's, and now they all do. And yes, Blake, alphas can't have Hensley's. Your father's not an alpha. Look at his face if you don't believe me."

He waved a hand at Prescott, who'd edged his way behind my father, eyes flicking around the room as if searching for an escape route.

"He's not an alpha," Dimitri went on implacably, every word exploding into the tense silence of the room like a bomb. "Or maybe he's partially alpha, some rare abnormality in his genes, the same one that gave him Hensley's, maybe. And they've been covering it up. With alpha magic, somehow. Fake alpha magic. And it's been making the Hensley's symptoms worse, hasn't it? That's why you're retiring now, Boyd. Because you can't keep it up anymore."

My father's breathing echoed too loudly, rough and uneven.

He'd deny it, wouldn't he? This couldn't possibly be true. Not after spending my whole life, *his* whole life, basing everything about our family and his expectations for me on his alpha status.

I glanced from Dimitri, eyes blazing and mouth set in a hard, grim line, to my father, his skin a blotchy mess of grayish pallor and purple flush, staring at Dimitri in horror.

He didn't like to show the alpha glow, because a real alpha kept himself under control.

The changes in his scent—probably as Prescott adjusted the strength of whatever magic he'd been using—that I'd dismissed as Dimitri's imagination.

The way he'd never been able to exert his dominance over me, not really, not with his voice and not with his presence—only with his anger and his belittling and his ability to cut me out of the company and the family if I didn't toe the line.

I couldn't draw a full breath, rage and agonized confusion churning in my belly, crippling in its intensity.

My whole life. A lie. His lie. Because he couldn't admit that he wasn't perfect.

"This is absurd," my mother said faintly. "Absolutely absurd. Insulting. Impossible. Boyd?"

But my father didn't answer. He sagged, swayed, and staggered to the nearest chair, falling into it like he'd been cut off at the knees.

With a cry, my mother lurched out of her chair and across to him, frantically calling his name, loosening his tie. She spun on Dimitri, eyes shining with tears. "You're killing him! These—your lies, you're killing him!"

"He's killing himself," Dimitri said heavily, not a trace of sympathy in his voice. No mercy. "And the only way he'll get better is if he cuts this shit out and retires. Gets some real treatment for the Hensley's symptoms."

"I can't believe this." A lost, pathetic whisper from across the room. Blake. When I looked at him, I almost didn't recognize my sneering, overconfident brother. He was staring at our parents, slack-jawed and trembling. For a moment I nearly empathized with him. His life had been shaped by their insanity as much as mine had, and neither of us had asked to be born. That burgeoning fellow-feeling evaporated as he said, "Brook's the one who's fucked up, not us. This isn't happening!"

Brook, not us. The three of them, the perfect family, marred only by their weak, pathetic, despised youngest member.

Even now, that was Blake's takeaway from all of this.

"I'm the only one of us who hasn't built his life on a lie." The words came out of my mouth before I even knew they'd formed in my mind. Because they were true. Yes, everything I'd endured at my family's hands had been because of a lie, but my education, my skills, my dedication—all of those were real. Mine, and no one could take them away from me. My voice didn't shake. It felt like someone else, someone braver and more sure, had taken over my body. Maybe I was the pod person. "He lied. She enabled it. And you—you never gave any of it a single thought beyond how it made your life easier."

Prescott spoke up at last, practically howling, "This wasn't my idea! He made me—"

"Shut the fuck up," Dimitri said, and Prescott went pale and shut the fuck up. "All of you shut the fuck up. Blake, get some water for your father and help your mom. Brook. Come here."

He didn't wait to see if Blake obeyed him, simply took me by the arm and towed me over to the far corner of the room. I let him lead me, half-blinded by shock, my feet simply stumbling along as directed. Dimitri put my back to the wall, and I slumped against it gratefully, desperate for the respite of something to lean on.

And for the heat and strength of my mate surrounding me, sheltering me from the scene across the room. For a moment, I let my eyes close, flashes of memory from my childhood flickering through my mind, every moment of it newly painful now that it'd been re-framed by the truth.

When I opened my eyes again, Dimitri had leaned down, eyes glowing and expression set. I didn't want to see anything else, and I fixed my gaze on him hungrily, using his face and his scent and his looming, protective body to shield me from the rest of the world. Beyond him, my family was melting down completely, arguing and crying.

Dimitri's powerful presence blocked them out.

"What do you want, Brook?" he asked softly. "You could walk away from all of this. Leave it behind and never have to see any of them again. Or you could take over, be the CEO. You need to tell me what you want."

A shaky laugh wavered out of my tight throat. "So you can get it for me?"

A smile teased at the corners of his mouth, even though his eyes were so bleak. "Yeah. So I can get it for you. That's what you hired me for, remember?"

Yeah. That's what I'd hired him for. I went cold all over, eyes prickling.

I'd hired him, and he'd quit his job soon enough, since that's what I was to him: a job.

But he wouldn't leave until he'd helped me get what I'd worked for. And I still wanted it, that was the thing. I really, truly did. I'd poured my heart and soul into Castelli Industries, as stupid as it sounded. Some of my colleagues, my employees, had worked just as hard to get where they were, and had supported me every step of the way despite the way my more senior colleagues treated me. Maybe I didn't care about the family name, but I did care about the reality it represented, all of the people who were so passionate about their work, and who depended on the company for their livelihoods.

I'd do better than my father. And I'd love every minute of it, because workaholic or not…I loved my job. Without him knocking me down every time I tried to stand on my own, I'd love it even more.

Almost as much as I loved Dimi—and I throttled that thought, forced it down so fast and hard it hurt.

That didn't matter. My feelings didn't matter, even though my chest ached, hollow and empty and cold.

"I want it," I said at last. Dimitri hadn't shown any signs of impatience, simply waiting for me to make my own decision. Not pushing, not trying to persuade me.

It was so fucking ironic that the only real alpha in the room—because apparently my father wasn't, and Blake certainly couldn't stand up to Dimitri—was the only one who didn't want to control my every thought and action.

"I want to be the CEO," I repeated, more strongly this time. "I know you think I'd be better off walking away. You probably think it's kind of a, a shallow aspiration, or maybe that it wasn't my own idea to begin with. But it's what I'm good at, and it's what I want."

Dimitri shook his head. "I don't think it's shallow. I've seen how hard you work. And I don't have an opinion about what would make you happy, Brook." His low voice had a tinge of real unhappiness of his own, and that made it hard to believe him. But he added, "No one gets to tell you what's best for you. I respect you enough to know you can make up your own mind."

That I believed, because he'd shown me over and over again that he did respect me. That he saw me as an equal. And maybe that unhappiness I'd heard in his tone, felt faintly through the bond, was simply because he knew what a shock I'd had. Maybe he was afraid I'd have another seizure after all.

But I knew I wouldn't. The seizures crept up on me when I felt powerless, when everything around me spiraled out of my control no matter how hard I tried or how diligently I worked.

This time, I knew what I needed to do.

"Come on," I said. "Let's deal with this and get the fuck out of here."

Dimitri nodded, and when he stood aside to let me out of the corner, I went ahead of him. He fell in behind me as if that had been his plan all along.

I faced the shambles of my family: my father still slumped in his chair and breathing hard; my mother hovering over him, looking like she'd aged ten years in the last ten minutes; Prescott, apparently trying to make himself invisible; and Blake, practically a different person without the veneer of his alpha posturing.

"Okay," I said, looking at each one of them in turn and then focusing on my father. "This is how it's going to be…"

Chapter 18

Don't Offer Me Anything Else

"Give him the keys," I said to the valet, and dropped into the passenger seat, leaning my head back and trying to calm the shaking of my hands and the rough, pounding vibration of my heartbeat.

Dimitri got in a second later, started the car, and pulled us out of the club's driveway without a word.

We'd made an announcement that unfortunately, my father had been taken ill, that it wasn't an emergency but that the family would be leaving, and that everyone was welcome to enjoy dinner and the club's amenities if they'd like.

And then we'd hightailed it out of there, leaving the rest of the "family" to figure it out their damn selves.

"We can't tell them he's ill!" my mother had wailed. "Alphas don't become ill. We can announce that you're the one who's sick. Everyone knows you're weak, that you—"

"We're not lying anymore," I'd said, more firmly than I'd ever have believed I'd be able to cut off my mother's ranting, fueled by a fresh wave of hurt and disgust. I'd always known she didn't care about me all that much. But she was my *mother*. And that wound wouldn't stop bleeding for a while, if ever, even if I could write my father and Blake off without a qualm. "We don't have to announce the whole truth to everyone in the world, but we're not lying anymore, and I'm not taking the blame for his bullshit."

And that was the end of that.

I'd told them my father would retire, and he'd promote me into his position as he did. And that I'd run the company without interference, paying them a generous—overgenerous, in fact—pension, out of which they could support Blake, on top of his own trust from our grandfather, if they wanted, but that I was done with him.

I hadn't needed to spell out the alternative. Dimitri had already taken care of that earlier, when he'd threatened to take the mic and spill all the family's secrets. He hadn't been bluffing, and they knew it.

My father nodded once, jerkily, and then closed his eyes.

Dimitri took my hand, and we left.

Just like that.

And now we were winding our way along the road home.

Wait, winding our way? The road home was mainly straight. I opened my eyes and saw not the lights of the suburbs, but the velvety shadows of a moonlit forest on the sides of the twisty road.

We came through the trees a moment later as the road emerged onto the side of the hill. Dimitri pulled over into a turnout overlooking the city, cutting the engine and slumping back in his seat with a sigh.

His hands worked at his throat, and then his tie went flying over his shoulder into the back seat to join its friends that he'd tossed back there every day after work.

Christ, I was going to miss him. I couldn't even begin to quantify how much.

My heart started pounding faster again. I'd gotten the other thing I wanted tonight, albeit in the worst possible way. Maybe I could convince him to stay. He still needed money, probably. He'd told me he needed the whole forty grand left over after he'd paid off his debts, and he'd tried to negotiate that extra twelve. If his mother needed some kind of specialized care, surgery, what have you…he might be eager to earn the money in a relatively easy way. I'd give it to him if he'd take it, of course. But I knew he wouldn't. He had too much pride. I tried not to feel guilty about the fact that his pride would put him in a position where he'd need to give me what I wanted from him.

"I need some air," Dimitri said, and popped his door open.

I followed, undoing my own tie and stuffing it in my pocket, taking up position next to him propped up on the hood of the car. Boise wasn't the biggest city in the world. Compared to real large cities, it was a speck on the map. But that only made it more beautiful, in my opinion. The Boise capitol building gleaming like a jewel, a few skyscrapers with their own interesting lighting schemes, and the scattershot glitter of the smaller buildings and the outlying suburbs, all of it surrounded by the soft darkness of mountains and a summer night. A cricket chirped nearby.

Well, this wasn't so bad. Especially with Dimitri lounging beside me, big and dangerous but at his ease, like a panther in a lazy mood.

Or maybe not quite at his ease. I glanced at him out of the corner of my eye, trying not to turn my head too much and let him know I was watching him. He'd leaned back on his hands, but the line of his shoulders and the angle of his head told me he hadn't really relaxed.

I couldn't ask him to stay, not without easing into it a little bit, anyway.

So I went with the second thing on my list. "When you were using my laptop, and on the phone all week? Were you working on figuring out what was up with my father?"

"Partly." He paused for a second. "I had some personal matters to attend to, too." Another pause. Jesus, this was like pulling teeth. I bit my lip to keep myself from prodding him. "But yeah. I did some research. Read everything I could find about Hensley's, all the stuff I hadn't dug up before, including the part where alphas can't even carry it, in addition to not being able to have it. By the way, that would've been good information to tell me to begin with, Brook."

My cheeks burned. Yeah, I remembered when I'd decided to keep that from him, and how I'd felt a little guilty about it even at the time, when I didn't know him yet. "It wasn't really relevant. I mean, it didn't matter. I'm not an alpha, so it didn't apply to me."

"Not relevant?" His voice rose, and I winced. "It was relevant. I might've put the pieces together a lot sooner about what the fuck was up with your father if you'd told me. To be fair, I should've kept reading on my own."

"You've done way more than you had any obligation to do," I said thickly, fresh guilt and shame and impending loss hitting me all at once. Fuck, I'd break down right here, the aftermath of adrenaline turning me into a shaky mess, and then Dimitri wouldn't want to stay. He'd want to run until he hit the ocean. "Thank you. For everything. I'm sorry I didn't tell you. I really didn't feel like airing more of someone else's secrets for no reason. Family loyalty, I guess." That last tasted as bitter as bile on my tongue, nearly as bitter as I felt.

"You're welcome. And I did make some calls, too, like you thought. Found a Russian shaman through some friends who helped me figure out what might be going on. Don't worry, I didn't give him anything identifiable."

If that shaman wanted to find us, connect the dots, he'd be able to, no matter how discreet Dimitri thought he'd been. Our mating had been in the local paper in the marriage announcements. An online search for Dimitri's name, a look at a photo of me in my un-werewolf-like glasses, my father's sudden retirement, which would be news by Monday…it wouldn't be that hard.

But I found that I didn't care. Fuck it. If my family's reputation suffered, that could be their fucking problem. My job would be to keep the company on an even keel and make sure it didn't affect us more than we could recover from.

And that'd be the type of challenge I'd face throughout my career, and hopefully rise above with grace. I smiled up at the stars. Okay, so I had one thing to look forward to.

"It doesn't matter that much," I said. "I'm grateful. Doubly grateful because you kept at it even after I blew you off. I was so focused on putting one foot in front of the other. Tunnel vision."

Another silence fell. "It wasn't just that. You believed him," he said at last, very quietly. "On some level, you bought into the bullshit. That you weren't good enough. That you needed an alpha to tell you what to do. If you'd been in the mindset of questioning him, you'd have figured it out a long time ago. You're smarter than me."

My cheeks glowed, luckily probably not noticeable in the faint moonlight—at least if he wasn't paying attention. But when I dared to turn my head, to really look at him, I found him already fully focused on me, eyes intent and gleaming.

For a moment, I lost myself completely. It'd almost happened before, his eyes drawing me in until I forgot to breathe, until the world faded away. This time, I had no defenses left.

I knew I had to get it together, present my case rationally and calmly. He needed money. I had it, and I'd have a lot more of it once my new salary kicked in. Fucking me satisfied him enough for a longer-term arrangement to work, right? And we got along well.

Better than well. Swimmingly, even. Living with him had been so easy, so pleasant, so *right*.

But I couldn't get the words out. Silvered by the moonlight, Dimitri held me in thrall with no more effort than it took him to exist. Black hair gleaming like part of the starry night sky, eyes like pewter, his hard features contrasting with the softness of the faint smile on his lips as he looked at me…

"Fucking hell," he rasped. "Brook." He reached out, cupping the side of my face, sliding his long fingers into my hair and caressing the corner of my mouth with his thumb. "I'm sorry. I can't not do this anymore."

That didn't compute, but before I could force my brain to function, he'd wrapped his other arm around my back, tipped me over it, and covered my mouth with his.

Dimitri's lips were hot on mine, firm and demanding, and he teased mine apart with his tongue, sweeping inside to claim me.

Not that it took much effort. I opened for him, welcoming him inside, electrified joy sparking through every nerve. He kissed me until I couldn't breathe, until I writhed in his arms, my cock stiff and aching and my body on fire, and held him so tightly in turn that I didn't think I'd ever be able to let him go. I climbed him like a tree, swinging my leg over so that I could straddle him, thighs spread wide around his, desperate to get his cock where I needed it. Inside me, fuck, I needed him inside me, filling me until I couldn't even moan anymore, until nothing existed but his knot stretching me open and making me his.

Dimitri slid his hand down under my ass to hold me up, the effortless strength of it driving me wild. He could take my weight with one arm, he could manhandle me any way he wanted, hold me down, own me…

When he broke the kiss, I whimpered and tried to chase his mouth, nipping at his lower lip. More, I needed more, I needed him to never, ever stop.

"Wait," he panted. "Brook, baby, wait. I need to—mmph," because I'd captured his mouth again. "Stop," and this time it came out a breathless gasp. He tugged me away, fingers tangled in my hair, and tipped my head back out of reach. His eyes dropped to my bared throat. "Fuck, that's not helping."

I licked my lips and moaned like the slut I'd become for him, and he shuddered under me, the hand on my ass gripping me almost painfully. "I don't want it to help. I want you to lay me out on the car and fuck me. Or the ground. I'm not picky."

"Yeah, well, I'm picky for you." He leaned in and kissed my throat, once, like he couldn't help it, his lips lingering. "I'll fuck you," he whispered against my skin, the vibrations shooting straight down to where I wanted him inside me. But he had me pinned—although that didn't help either. "I'll fuck you all night, all day, all fucking week without stopping. But you need to tell me what I am to you, first."

"What you—oh, fuck, Dimitri—you're my mate. My alpha."

He bit down, snarling, so rigid under me he felt like stone. The pain lanced through me, so much headier than pure pleasure.

When he let me go, he lapped at my bruised skin. "I am your mate," he growled between licks. "Fuck. Fine. I'm your fucking alpha, Brook, and I'm not going anywhere. You fucking understand? Call me your alpha one more time, and I'm never leaving you."

He was never leaving me.

Not because I'd offered him another chunk of money, but because he wanted me. *Me*, Brook, with all my imperfections.

"Alpha," I gasped, and he surged up, carrying me with him as he moved quickly away from the car. I wrapped my legs around his waist and let him jounce us wherever he wanted to go, kissing him at the same time, laughing when he tripped and cursed, because everything was pure joy, fizzing through my veins like champagne.

I didn't realize what he had in mind until he let me down, mouth still molded to mine, nibbling at my lips and chasing me, and stripped off his jacket.

He tossed it on the grass and then toppled me down after it, and I squawked and fought him. "Dimitri! That's a custom tailored jack—mmm," and I forgot about the tailoring and everything else in that possessive, devouring kiss.

It was a good thing I'd lost interest in the state of our tuxes, because he tore mine off of me with a combination of claws, single-minded determination, and brute strength, seams popping and fabric ripping and buttons flying.

I didn't even have a chance to worry about the lack of lube. Dimitri shoved my legs up and open and dived in, eating me out until I screamed and tugged at his hair, coming all over myself.

He swiped up my come, slicked his cock with it, and slid home.

I stared up at him, transfixed, gasping for breath. Silhouetted by the pale moonlight, muscles straining, he could've been the stunt double for that demon lover in the book I might or might not have read to ragged shreds. His eyes glowed brighter than the stars, pure gold in the darkness, and fixed on me with overwhelming intensity.

"You're really not leaving? Once I'm—once you've finished the job?" I whispered. He'd told me so, but—shit, maybe it was only for the promised stipend after all? If he knotted me now, held me close to his heart while I called him my mate and my alpha and spilled my longing into the night, and then wanted me for my money after all, it might break me. "Why do you want to stay? I was going to offer to—ask you to stay. Offer you whatever you wanted, but—"

"Shut up," he growled, and put a hand over my mouth to ensure it. I kissed his palm, and his eyes brightened and darkened all at once, shining gold over pupil-blown black. "If you offer me money again, I'll—fuck."

"You'll what?" I mumbled into his hand, wriggling on the thick cock buried in me, smiling when his eyes shut for a moment and he slammed his hips against me helplessly.

"I'll nothing," he said, after he'd sucked in a deep breath. "That's the problem. I won't hurt you. I won't leave. I won't stop cooking for you. I got nothing." His chest heaved, and he opened his eyes, fixing me with that gaze again. "I only want you. That's it. Don't offer me anything else."

"You have me, you have me, always, now fuck me. Dimitri!" He thrust so hard he shoved me off the jacket and onto the grass, damp and prickly against my spine. I didn't care. "Harder, I'm yours, God, please, you feel so good inside me…"

I trailed off into an incoherent litany of begging and endearments and demands, and Dimitri answered each one by taking me apart, stroke after stroke, filling every empty place in me, body and soul.

By the time I came again as his knot forced the orgasm out of me, the words flowing out of my mouth had gone beyond any possibility of control.

"I love you," I gasped.

He didn't reply, simply groaning his own pleasure into my ear as he shook in my arms, hips jerking in a staccato rhythm, his knot punching into me with every movement.

What I'd said sank in as my heartbeat started to slow, as I gazed up at the stars, Dimitri's panting breaths hot on my neck and the night air cool on my legs where they weren't heated by his. I stroked his back through the shirt he hadn't managed to tear off all the way, tracing his muscles with my fingertips.

Dimitri lifted his head. I didn't want to meet his eyes, but I had to when he took my chin in his hand and turned me to him, gently but inexorably.

"Did I just hear what I thought I heard?" I couldn't read his tone at all, as if he was keeping himself neutral through sheer force of will.

I swallowed hard and nodded.

The smile that broke out across his face lit him up more than any moonlight ever could've, brighter than his eyes. "I love you too. In case you were wondering. Anyway, if you were, don't ever wonder again. I love you, and you're mine."

No one had ever told me that before. No one, not my parents, not a boyfriend. No one at all.

Dimitri had been worth the wait, because those words in his deep, raspy voice flowed into me, around me, soothing and comforting me in ways I'd never even imagined.

Would this be what my life would be like from now on? His, and only his, and never alone again? Taking the job I'd worked so hard for, finally getting the recognition I deserved for all those hours and weeks and years of slaving away…but the vindication of that paled in comparison to this.

I shimmied my hips, biting my lips against a moan when it rubbed his knot against all kinds of interesting places.

"I think you've staked your claim," I said hoarsely, unable to find words for everything in my mind and my heart. "I don't think I'm going anywhere." And then, helplessly, because I couldn't keep it in, "I love you."

"Never going to get tired of hearing that." He nuzzled my cheek, nipped at my jaw, licked and nibbled me until I squirmed and laughed and tried—and failed—to shove him off.

"Fine! I love you I love you I love—stop tickling me—Dimitri!" I protested as he went for the curve of my throat again.

We didn't manage to get up off the ground, collect the grass-stained remnants of two beautifully tailored suits, and go home for another hour. Or more? It hardly mattered, because the moon and the stars wheeled above, and the crickets chirped, and an owl hooted at us, and we had nowhere else to be besides together.

I spent the drive stark naked with half a jacket draped over my lap.

Dimitri laughed at me, even though it was his fault, grin flashing in the darkness.

And then we went home together, and he carried me over the threshold just because he could, and from there—straight to bed.

My mate. My alpha.

And I didn't do any work at all on Sunday.

Epilogue
I'm Ready

Three months later

The last of the moving boxes barely fit in the truck, something groaning ominously behind them as Dimitri gave a final shove to get them in.

"Watch it, all the dishes are back there!"

He turned his head to glare at me over his shoulder. "They're ugly dishes, baby. Besides, my mom's bringing hers. You really think we're going to be eating anything in our own kitchen after she takes over? Get real."

"But she has her own cottage!" I protested. "She's not going to cook us three meals a day."

Dimitri burst out laughing. "Uh-huh. More like four. Or five, after she starts in about how you're too skinny."

I glanced down at my perfectly normal, occasionally-gym-honed body in dismay. "I'm really not."

"She thinks I'm too skinny, let alone you." Dimitri gave a hard yank on the sliding door of the truck, and it rattled down and settled in with a satisfying thump and click. Something else settled inside the truck with another creak, and I winced. Fuck it. The door was closed. Too late now. "Seriously, Brook. You don't understand Russian moms yet, but you will. We'll never cook again. And she's a much, much better cook than I am."

I went a little misty-eyed thinking about the unimaginable quantities—and quality—of food she'd prepared for us when we visited her for the first time, two weeks after the showdown at the mating-reception-that-wasn't. I was shocked by how well she navigated the kitchen in her wheelchair, apparently not slowed down in the slightest. Dimitri had finally told me how she'd been injured: his father, drunk and careless, too confident in his own werewolf healing to worry about his wife's vulnerable humanity.

Dimitri had been typically tight-lipped about the details, though I trusted him to tell me more as time went on, just as I knew he truly did trust me. But he had trouble opening up. That was okay. I'd be there when he did.

At least I finally understood the root of his fierce protectiveness when I showed any symptoms of Hensley's. Dimitri's father had neglected his injured mate, scoffed at her for her weakness, and then finally fucked off back to Russia—with, it sounded like, some none-too-gentle prodding from his twenty-year-old alpha son. Reading between the lines, Dimitri had put him on the plane with his claws at his father's jugular, confiscating all his available cash at the same time to use for Nadia's care.

Another, very expensive, experimental surgery might get her walking again, and when Dimitri had found me researching hospitals one night when I should've been working on the company's ten-year strategy plan instead, he hadn't said a word: just pulled me out of my chair, kissed me until my head spun, and gone downstairs to make me a snack.

I didn't need him to thank me. Nadia had embraced me like a second son, fed me, and apparently spent hours on the phone bragging about her handsome CEO son-in-law to all of her friends.

Yeah, I was team Nadia.

And Dimitri's sister—the real one, not the pregnant one I'd invented without realizing how close I'd come to the truth—wasn't bad either, a smaller, slightly less dangerous version of her older brother. Slightly. I wasn't about to do anything to piss her off.

And she made incredible pastry.

Which brought me back to the food. "Yeah," I said, sounding a little dreamy. "She really is a better cook than you. They both are."

"That's the gratitude I get," he said, laughing, and yanked me into his arms, kissing me breathless. "You ready to go? Blow this popsicle stand?"

I took a long, last look at the house my family had chosen for me. I hadn't hated it a lot of the time, although I'd definitely nursed a simmering distaste. And I'd liked it a lot more with Dimitri in it;

he'd even warmed up to the couch he despised so much. "It looks a lot better with you naked all over it," he'd said. And he'd been right.

But I had no regrets. We'd bought our own place a couple of miles away, closer to work in a quiet little rural suburb. Three bedrooms in the main house, and two in the one-story cottage out back, now fully remodeled in a big hurry to accommodate Dimitri's mom and sister. Dimitri would be driving down to Arizona to get them at the end of the week.

"I'm ready." And I was. So very, very ready to live out of the shadow of my family, to welcome a new family into my life, to make the best of every moment.

Before, I'd worked because I didn't have anything else.

Now, I'd be working to support the people who loved me, who'd support me in turn.

"Me too." Dimitri wrapped his arms around me, nuzzled my neck, and got me all hot and bothered within seconds. Dammit, there wasn't room in the truck to do anything about it. "We still have to christen most of the new house. With furniture, this time. I still feel bad about the rug burn."

"No, you don't."

He laughed and nipped at my ear. "No, I don't. But I'll bend you over the kitchen counter this time to save your back."

"So romantic," I groused, but I couldn't suppress my smile— or the stiffening of my cock, which loved the idea of the kitchen counter.

And loved Dimitri as much as I did.

My fake mate. My unlikely alpha. My Dimitri, as imperfect as I was and impossibly perfect for me at the same time.

We untangled ourselves, climbed in the truck, and set off for our new home and our new life, hand in hand.

The End

Thanks for reading, and I hope you enjoyed Brook and Dimitri's story!

The Alpha Contract stands alone, but Brook's alpha cousin Drew's HEA with his human mate can be found in *Lost Touch*, the previous book in the Mismatched Mates series.

Acknowledgments

Thank you so much to Alessandra Hazard and Kai Butler for reading the first few chapters of this book in its early stages, and thanks twice to Alessandra for reading it all the way through in the later stages too!

As always, I owe a great deal to my intrepid beta reader, Amy Pittel. Amy always has the funniest comments. I love reading them as much as I hope she enjoys reading my books in the first place.

Special shout-outs go to Brandy, who lent her name to Brook's genetic condition, and to Barbara K., who inspired "Creek," Blake's terrible nickname for his brother.

Thank you to everyone for reading!

Get in Touch

I love hearing from readers! Find me at eliotgrayson.com, where you can get more info about my books and also sign up for my newsletter or contact me directly. You can also find out about my other books on Amazon, or join my Facebook readers' group to get more frequent updates. Thanks for reading!

Also by Eliot Grayson

Mismatched Mates:
The Alpha's Warlock
Captive Mate
A Very Armitage Christmas
The Alpha Experiment
Lost and Bound
Lost Touch

Blood Bonds:
First Blood
Twice Bitten

Goddess-Blessed:
The Replacement Husband
The Reluctant Husband
Yuletide Treasure

Portsmouth:
Like a Gentleman
Once a Gentleman

Santa Rafaela:
The One Decent Thing
A Totally Platonic Thing

Deven and the Dragon

Brought to Light

Undercover

The Wrong Rake

Made in the USA
Columbia, SC
15 December 2024

49453512R00105